the further adventures of

SHERLOCK HOLMES

SHERLOCK HOLMES VS. DRACULA

AVAILABLE NOW FROM TITAN BOOKS
THE FURTHER ADVENTURES OF SHERLOCK HOLMES SERIES:

THE ECTOPLASMIC MAN
Daniel Stashower

THE WAR OF THE WORLDS
Manly Wade Wellman & Wade Wellman

THE SCROLL OF THE DEAD
David Stuart Davies

THE STALWART COMPANIONS
H. Paul Jeffers

THE VEILED DETECTIVE
David Stuart Davies

THE MAN FROM HELL
Barrie Roberts

SÉANCE FOR A VAMPIRE
Fred Saberhagen

THE SEVENTH BULLET
Daniel D. Victor

THE WHITECHAPEL HORRORS
Edward B. Hanna

DR. JEKYLL AND MR. HOLMES
Loren D. Estleman

THE GIANT RAT OF SUMATRA
Richard L. Boyer

THE PEERLESS PEER
Philip José Farmer

THE STAR OF INDIA
Carole Buggé

THE WEB WEAVER
Sam Siciliano

THE TITANIC TRAGEDY
William Seil

SHERLOCK HOLMES VS. DRACULA

THE ADVENTURE OF THE SANGUINARY COUNT

LOREN D. ESTLEMAN

TITAN BOOKS

THE FURTHER ADVENTURES OF SHERLOCK HOLMES
SHERLOCK HOLMES VS. DRACULA
Print edition ISBN: 9781781161425
E-book edition ISBN: 9781781161432

Published by
Titan Books
A division of Titan Publishing Group Ltd
144 Southwark St
London
SE1 0UP

First edition: November 2012
10 9 8 7 6 5 4 3 2 1

Visit our website: **www.titanbooks.com**

A CIP catalogue record for this title is available from the British Library.

Printed in the USA.

To Sir Arthur Conan Doyle, creator of the Sherlock Holmes stories, and to Bram Stoker, author of Dracula, from whose fertile brains sprang the two most enduring characters in fiction, this volume is gratefully dedicated.

"This agency stands flat-footed upon the ground, and there it must remain. The world is big enough for us. No ghosts need apply."

SHERLOCK HOLMES,
AS QUOTED IN "THE ADVENTURE OF THE SUSSEX VAMPIRE"

"How often have I said to you that when you have eliminated the impossible, whatever remains, *however improbable*, must be the truth?"

SHERLOCK HOLMES,
AS QUOTED IN "THE SIGN OF FOUR"

Foreword

Da Vinci's final notebook, the wreckage of Amelia Earhart's last airplane, the civilization of Atlantis–none of these long-lost items holds more value for the student of history than the famed "battered tin dispatch-box" in which Dr. John H. Watson claimed to have stored the records of a number of cases he shared with Sherlock Holmes and never published. Surely it is there that we will find the shocking particulars of the adventure of the giant rat of Sumatra, "a story for which the world is not yet prepared," and read at last about the politician, the lighthouse, and the trained cormorant, two of the many problems which Watson bandies about with the expertise of a professional fan dancer, giving us just enough of a glimpse of the good parts to make us whistle for more. We know for a fact, because Watson has told us, that the twin mysteries of the disappearance of the cutter *Alicia* and of Isadora Persano, who was found "stark staring mad" in the presence of a matchbox containing "a remarkable worm said to be unknown to science," await us beneath that battered lid. What a shame, and what a loss to the world, that all of these case histories are believed to have perished when, during the

London Blitz, a German bomber pilot with no feeling for posterity deposited his load onto the bank of Cox & Co. in Charing Cross, where the dispatch-box was kept. War was never more devastating than this!

Still, there is hope. Just as there are thousands of attics and cellars in Italy, any one of which night hold Leonardo's wonders, and just as the ocean may yet give up the secrets of Lady Lindy and Atlantis, so it is possible–even probable–that Watson's treasures were transported after his death in 1940 to some safer place than wartorn London, patiently waiting to be discovered. It is this kind of hope that keeps the collector going when others have given up. Indeed, without such hope I would not be writing this now, for it was while I was engaged in tracking down the good doctor's dispatch-box that I stumbled upon the material which follows this Foreword.

Some backtracking is necessary. Since what little we know about Sherlock Holmes's background comes almost wholly as a result of a handful of oblique references to his family when the detective was in a discursive mood, the scattered places in which Watson recorded these offhand comments are of enormous importance in unraveling the mystery of what happened to the unpublished accounts. In "The Greek Interpreter," Holmes, in addition to astounding his friend with the revelation that he has a brother whose deductive skills surpass his own, dwells briefly upon his ancestors, country squires "who appear to have led much the same life as is natural to their class." In the same paragraph we learn that his grandmother was "the sister of Vernet, the French artist." The question as to whether or not the detective was indulging in mere braggadocio seems to be answered by Watson's statement some ten or twelve years later that he had sold his practice to another physician by the name of Verner who turned out to be a distant relative of Holmes's. The names are too similar to be coincidental.

At any rate, it was the name Verner which caught my attention while I was scanning the obituary pages of the Detroit *News* early last July. It was a fairly short item beneath the heading DEATHS ELSEWHERE, and read as follows:

LONDON, ONTARIO (UPI)–Creighton T. Verner, believed by many to have been the last living relative of legendary British detective Sherlock Holmes, died here today at the age of 98. He was found early this morning seated in an armchair in the living room of his home at 4417 Royal Street by his housekeeper. His death was attributed to natural causes.

Verner, a retired physician, left England in 1916 following the death of his only son Victor in the trenches of World War I and never returned. The last forty years of his life were spent in the modest four-room cottage in which he died. No funeral services are planned.

As a Sherlockian in good standing with the local affiliate of the New York-based Baker Street Irregulars, I was naturally saddened by the demise of this last link with the Holmes legend. I was not, however, sufficiently moved to make the hundred-mile journey to view either the dead man's remains or the soulless little dwelling in which he spent his declining years. It was this item, culled from a later issue of the *News*, which changed my mind:

LONDON, ONTARIO (UPI)–Sherlock Holmes scholars from all over the world are expected to be in attendance next Monday when the estate of Dr. Creighton T. Verner will be auctioned off by the Canadian government to pay his back taxes. Verner, who passed away last week at the age of 96 [*sic*]; was a distant cousin of the world's first consulting detective.

Among the items scheduled to go on the block are a number of the famous "commonplace books" in which Holmes pasted the reference material he gleaned from whatever periodicals he could lay his hands upon; the Persian slipper, now motheaten and encrusted with mold, which once held the sleuth's tobacco; a collection of charred pipes; and miscellaneous articles believed to have belonged both to Holmes and to Dr. John H. Watson, his biographer. In addition, several pieces of antique furniture will be up for sale.

The auction, which will begin at 9:00 a.m. EDT before Verner's home at 4417 Royal Street in *London...*

I cannot remember if I finished reading the article before I began packing. The next morning, my car loaded with enough clothes and supplies to last me a week, I crossed over to Canada via the Ambassador Bridge and drove nonstop to London. All the way there my thoughts were centered upon one question: Could the "miscellaneous articles" mentioned in the newspaper story include the elusive dispatch-box?

The answer was no. Varied as were the items which had filled an unused room of the tiny cottage for forty years, from an intricately carved chiffonier of inestimable value to a number of worthless chipped enamel "thunder-mugs," the tin box was not among them. Even Holmes's and Watson's personal effects, of no great value except to the collector, were denied me due to the ridiculously high bids they drew from the rabid auctiongoers. Disappointed, but nonetheless determined not to go home empty-handed, I bid five dollars for a dusty cardboard carton of junk from the last century, got it, and without bothering to examine its contents, slid it into the back seat of my car and drove straight home.

It was not until the next morning, after I had had a decent night's sleep, that I had a chance to look at my purchase more closely and discovered a tattered sheaf of papers crammed between one of the cardboard flaps and the inside of the box. That it had not received close attention from someone before me I blamed upon the nearly indecipherable handwriting which filled the gray pages. It took me over an hour to get through the preface and the first chapter, and once I realized what it was, my breakfast, lunch, and dinner were forgotten as I hastened to read the manuscript all the way to the end.

The skeptic will no doubt wonder, and he would be quite right to do so, why this account was not published when it was written some eighty years ago. It is my contention that Watson fully intended to submit it to his publishers, but that he was talked out of it by his ever-discreet companion on the grounds that it would be better for all concerned if it never saw print, since the public had already accepted Bram Stoker's version as fiction, and there was no sense in alarming Victorian society's sensibilities. What, I have often asked myself, was Watson's reaction? Did he, after all the work he put into setting it down, turn it over to Holmes with express and anatomical instructions as to what he was a physician, subject to the cryptic scrawl that is common to do with it? Probably he expressed himself more delicately. In any case, I believe that he did something of the sort, but that the detective did not follow his advice and simply stuck it away among his other records, where it was forgotten. When he died early in the first third of this century it was sent to his cousin along with all his other possessions. That Verner never threw anything away is something for which we can all be thankful.

This hypothesis may also be stretched to answer another damaging argument against the manuscript's authenticity. Readers of "The Adventure of the Sussex Vampire," which experts agree took place in 1897–the year in which Watson wrote the present chronicle–will note that Sherlock Holmes was quite emphatic in his disavowal of any belief in vampires and the supernatural, referring to it as "rubbish." I believe that this statement is fiction. If the detective team agreed that no one should learn of Holmes's involvement in the Dracula affair, it follows that the Baker Street sleuth would be expected officially to pooh-pooh the possibility of such things existing.

If, however, it was not fiction, then perhaps the detective was being ironic. He was no doubt still chafing over Stoker's omission of his and Watson's names from the official account of the case, published not long before (see Watson's Preface), and may have been inclined to treat yet another vampire challenge with less than his usual professional calm. There may be other explanations, but these two seem the most obvious.

Herewith, then, is "The Adventure of the Sanguinary Count," much as Dr. Watson set it down nearly a century ago. It must be remembered that the stalwart veteran of the Afghanistan campaign was a physician, subject to the cryptic scrawl that is common to the members of his profession, and that some passages have defied the efforts of the editor to translate them into legibility. Where these appear I have been forced to substitute, and although I have done my best to anticipate what he had to say and to emulate his style in setting it down, I have few illusions but that some erudite individual will seize upon the inevitable inconsistencies as proof that the entire manuscript is a forgery. To these charges I can only respond by quoting the good doctor's own words, from "A Study in Scarlet":

"What ineffable twaddle!"

Loren D. Estleman
Dexter, Michigan
April 30, 1978

Preface

Before I begin my narrative, I feel that it is my duty to set the reader straight upon a number of erroneous statements made recently regarding the events therein described. I refer in particular to a spurious monograph which has enjoyed a certain amount of popularity since it first appeared some four months ago, authored by an Irishman by the name of Bram Stoker, and entitled *Dracula.*

To begin with, the book, which purports to be a collection of letters and journals written by some of the principal figures involved, completely ignores the part which Sherlock Holmes (and, to a lesser extent, myself) played in bringing that affair to its successful conclusion among the snow-capped peaks of Transylvania. Although Holmes does not agree, it is my belief that Professor Van Helsing induced Stoker to deliberately falsify the facts where our line of investigation transected his, in order to build up his own reputation as a supernatural detective, and to invent entire episodes to explain the discrepancies. That I do not make these charges lightly will be borne out by what follows.

A case in point: As set down by Stoker, the professor's friend Dr. John Seward claims that the "Bloofer Lady" (so she was named by the newspapers) was destroyed during the hours of daylight on September 29. In reality, it was on the night of the twenty-eighth, or, to be more precise, early on the morning of the twenty-ninth, that Lord Godalming pounded the sanctifying stake into her unclean breast, thus freeing her of the vampire's curse. A further example of the author's and Van Helsing's duplicity takes place when the professor mentions that the *Czarina Catherine* left Doolittle's Wharf in London bound for Varna, on the Black Sea, with the Count aboard on the afternoon of October fourth, when even a halfhearted perusal of the shipping schedules for that period will show that it was not until the following morning that the ship sailed and that its port of departure was Whitby, in Yorkshire, and not London. As to the reason for this alteration of the facts, and for the fanciful tale which Stoker dreamed up to cover his indiscretion, the only solution I can render is that this was merely another attempt to discredit any claim which Holmes or I might make regarding our breakneck pursuit of the vampire throughout the night of the fourth.

Lest I emerge from these pages a complete simpleton in the eyes of my readers, some explanation is necessary regarding the knowledge of vampire lore in England in 1890. Now that everyone who reads has become conversant with the meaning of such things as garlic and wooden stakes and the presence of tiny wounds upon the jugular, I suppose that my failure to recognise these apparent trifles for what they were will brand me obtuse. But the fact remains that, before the appearance of Stoker's abomination, such things were as foreign to the average British subject as are the rites of tree worship as practised among some primitive tribes. I dare say that fewer than one in a hundred Londoners could have seen the truth, as Holmes did, when faced with a jumble of such seemingly unrelated oddities.

The account which follows is the correct one. I have double-checked the copious notes which I took at the time of the events I describe and am reasonably certain of their accuracy. In order that the reader who is interested in substantiating my narrative may do so without confusion, I have in this case abandoned my customary practice of substituting fictitious names in place of those of the actual participants, and have clouded none of the pertinent facts, so indignant am I at the injustice which some chroniclers will do in the name of art. To those who would defend Stoker, I refer them to the section in his book dealing with the Bloofer Lady, in which he is unable to decide whether the colour of her attire was black or white. It is a distinction which both he and Professor Van Helsing seem to have difficulty in determining.

John H. Watson, M.D.
London, England
September 15, 1897

Chapter One

The Death Ship

I need hardly consult my notebook for 1890 to recall that it was in August of that year that my friend Mr. Sherlock Holmes, with some slight assistance by me, set out to unravel the single most terrible and bone-chilling mystery which it has been my privilege to relate. Those who are familiar with these somewhat incoherent accounts may remember that I have made much the same observation upon more than one occasion, most notably in the case of Miss Susan Cushing of Croydon and the grisly package she received through the mail, elsewhere recorded as "The Adventure of the Cardboard Box." In my defence, I can only state that the affair I am about to set down is the only one in which I have Holmes's complete agreement concerning the singular nature of the chain of events that led us, in spirit if not in body, from his comfortable quarters in Baker Street to the bleak, snow-swept landscape of one of the easternmost provinces of the European continent.

The heat wave which at the beginning of August had emptied London of all those fortunate souls who could afford to leave for the cooler temperatures of the country had just broken. My temper being of the sort that vanishes as the mercury climbs–despite a higher than average tolerance to such hardships gained through an extended sojourn in India–I had sought to make use of the break by taking the air and thus give my long-suffering wife a chance to forgive the unreasonable misanthrope with whom she had been living for the past few days. It was late morning, then, when I chanced to drop in upon my friend in his Bohemian lodgings and found him hard at work imparting in formation into one of those commonplace books upon which so many criminals would dearly love to lay their hands.

"You are right, Watson," said Holmes, breaking a silence of some minutes which had settled in after greetings had been exchanged and I had ensconced myself in the chair opposite him. "Dr. Grimesby Roylott was indeed a murderer and a bully, who no doubt richly deserved his fate."

"No doubt," I echoed, and then realising with a start that he had just responded to my inmost thought, I came forward in my chair and stared at him in disbelief.

"My dear Holmes!" I cried. "This is too much! Am I to assume that you have transcended the bounds of reason and are now on a level with the palmsters and mind readers?"

He chuckled and leaned back, filling his cherry-wood pipe with shag from the toe end of the Persian slipper he kept always within reach. "Nothing so mysterious as that, I fear," he said, between puffs. "There is no magic at 221B, unless one counts the ability to observe and make deductions based upon those observations."

"But I have done nothing that could be observed!" said I. "I have been a fixture since I sat down!"

"No man is a fixture, Watson. He may think he is, and yet by a careful observation of his unconscious gestures, of his expression, and of the direction in which his eyes wander, a close reasoner would find rare instances in which he could not divine the mental processes of a man deep in thought. For example, as you were assuming your present seat, I noted that your attention was momentarily claimed by my little monograph on poisons, lying upon yonder table. It is open to the chapter which deals with vipers and their venom. Now, since our only brush with such a means of death occurred in the case of the swamp adder used by the villainous Dr. Roylott in the attempted murder of his stepdaughter–an imaginative account of which I believe you are planning to publish under the title 'The Adventure of the Speckled Band'–it was not so difficult to surmise that your thoughts were turned in that direction. My suspicions along these lines became confirmed when I saw the look of disgust and revulsion which crossed your face at this point. When that expression turned to one of righteous anger, I was certain that I was on the right track. Whereupon I agreed with you that Dr. Roylott was a bounder of the worst sort and was pleased to see by your reaction that my reasoning was sound."

"Holmes, Holmes." I shook my head, smiling. "Again I must state that you do yourself a disservice by explaining your methods. The effect would be so much greater if you left your subjects in the dark."

"And your chronicles of my little exploits would as a result be shelved alongside the fanciful works of Monsieur Verne and the Brothers Grimm. But see what you think of this telegram. It arrived this morning during breakfast."

I took the scrap of paper he proffered and read:

WOULD LIKE TO CONSULT YOU IN THE MATTER OF THE
LEAD COLUMN IN THIS MORNING'S DAILYGRAPH.
THOMAS C. PARKER
WHITBY, YORKS.

"It appears to be a legitimate request for your services," I said, handing back the wire.

"So it does."

"Have you read the article he mentions?"

"I sent down for it after receiving the wire. The problem therein reported presents one or two interesting facets, and I think we should both profit from learning more of the particulars. I assume your practice will make no demands upon your time for the next hour or so?"

"None whatsoever. The heat wave has seen to it that most of my patients are out of the city."

"Excellent!" said he, closing the scrapbook and returning it to its place upon the shelf beside the others. "For here, unless I am very much mistaken, is Mr. Parker's tread upon the stair."

No sooner had my friend finished speaking than there was a rap at the door. "Come in!" Holmes called.

Our visitor was a young man, six-and-twenty at the outside, with a beardless face nearly as narrow as Holmes's but less sharp, and dominated by a pair of large and watery blue eyes. He wore a lightweight suit of a pale grey and a billycock hat, which he snatched off immediately upon entering; in so doing he revealed a prematurely bald head ringed by a fringe of hair the colour of rust. "Mr. Holmes, I think?" he said, looking at my friend.

"I am he," Holmes acknowledged, rising and extending. his hand for the visitor to take. "And you, I take it, are Mr. Thomas C. Parker of Whitby. Allow me to introduce my friend and colleague, Dr. Watson. Sit down, Mr. Parker, and bask in the warmth of London in the summertime."

"You have read the item to which I referred in my wire?" asked Parker, assuming the seat which I had newly vacated.

Holmes nodded but said nothing.

"I am its author."

"I am aware of that."

"Indeed! And how?"

Sherlock Holmes, hands in the pockets of his old purple dressing-gown, smiled condescendingly down at his guest. "I knew you were a journalist from the moment you entered the room. The ink stains upon the insides of the index finger and thumb of your right hand, together with the bulge in your breast pocket, which I perceive to be created by a notebook residing there, told me that you spend much of your time writing. That you are seldom off your feet is borne out by the run-down appearance of your heels. Journalism is the only profession I can think of which combines such energy with the more placid activity of putting pen to paper. I thought it likely that you were the same journalist who had penned the rather interesting account to which you directed me. But all this is elementary. Pray tell us what is on your mind. It is obvious that your mission is not an unpleasant one personally, for your knock at the door was not the knock of a worried man." Upon which cryptic statement my friend lounged into his big armchair and studied the man opposite him from beneath languidly drooping lids.

For some seconds Mr. Parker eyed my friend with the sort of professional interest shared only by the scribblers who work for the daily journals and chroniclers such as myself. Presently, however, his expression became businesslike. "Mr. Holmes, I have been authorised by my editors to extend to you a fee in the name of *The Dailygraph* in return for providing us with the solution to the mystery which took place in Whitby harbour at midnight last night."

My friend made an impatient gesture with his left hand, as if to flick away a persistent fly which was causing him bother. "We shall discuss such things as my fee later. For now, I wish to hear a summary of the facts as you know them in your own words, independent of the restraining hand of some over-cautious editor."

The journalist nodded agreement and began his singular narrative, which I will endeavour to set down exactly as he delivered it. It ran as follows:

"Until yesterday evening," he informed us, "the weather in Whitby since the beginning of August has been much like that which you are now enjoying in London. Just before midnight, however, and with a suddenness that is not normally experienced upon the coast, the air became so oppressively still that even the most ignorant of city-dwellers could be naught but certain that a storm was approaching.

"There is a great flat reef in Whitby harbour which has spelled doom for many a vessel whose master was unaware of its presence. With this in mind, the Royal Navy has installed a searchlight atop the East Cliff for the purpose of guiding harbouring craft through the narrow alley that affords the only safe passage from the open sea into the dock area. Last night I was assigned by my editor to accompany the workers who were labouring to put the light into operating order and report upon the project's worth for the benefit of the shipping companies whose paid advertisements are *The Dailygraph*'s main staple; This promised to be a boring as well as an uncomfortable task, and so I was not in the most receptive of moods when I arrived on the cliff's summit just as the bell in the church tower was striking the hour of twelve.

"The final chime had scarcely begun to fade when the storm struck in all its terrible fury. The wind howled like a pack of ravenous wolves and rain lashed the cliff with the force of an explosion. My father was a correspondent during the Franco-Prussian War, Mr. Holmes, and from what I know of his experiences, a hail of lead from Napoleon's Gatling guns was no more terrible a sight than the spectacle of all that water pounding at the wall of the cliff as if it were trying to bring it crashing down into the harbour. The workers had all they could do to hold their footing as they strained to swing the big searchlight into position so that it could do some good. At one point I even lent my own shoulder to the task, and suffered a severely pulled muscle as a result of my exertions. I am not exaggerating when I tell you that a great sigh was heaved by all concerned when the light was lit and its bold yellow beam shone out through the rain and the darkness.

"In the next moment, however, that sigh was strangled in our throats when we saw what that beam revealed.

"Ghastly yellow in the circle of light, a foreign schooner with all its sails set was racing inexorably towards the murderous reef!"

"Foreign, you say?" Holmes interrupted. "What were her colours?"

"She flew none, but her hull was unmistakably Russian in design."

"I see. Pray go on with your narrative."

"The supreme folly of the captain and crew in failing to furl the sails at the first sign of a squall was, I am certain, uppermost in everyone's mind at that point, for now there was no force on earth that would prevent that fragile wooden hull from being dashed to splinters against that natural obstacle and all its hands from being flung into the merciless sea. We braced ourselves for the ear-splitting crash we believed was inevitable. And then a curious thing happened.

"Just when all seemed lost, the wind, which until now had been raging in an easterly direction, suddenly and abruptly shifted to the northeast, and the schooner glided into the harbour with the ease of a book being slid into its allotted space upon a shelf. This occurrence was so unlike the disaster we had been expecting that I doubt any of us believed what our eyes had told us. It seemed to all of us upon the East Cliff then that perhaps there was something to that biblical quotation about the Lord looking after fools and drunkards. I hope I am not boring you with all these details, Mr. Holmes, for I am trying to impress upon you what it was like to witness this event."

"On the contrary, it is a most lucid and informative account. What occurred then?"

"It seems that it was a night for disillusionment," continued our guest sadly. "Once again our feelings of joy were premature, for, as the schooner slid past, the searchlight fell upon a horrendous sight: that of a corpse lashed to the helm, its drooping head swinging to and fro with each motion of the ship. So spine-chilling was this unexpected vision that we forgot to swing the light, and the vessel with its grotesque cargo slid from view into the blackness of the night. By the time we recovered enough to act, there was a wrenching sound, followed by a crash, and presently the light revealed what I think most of us already suspected–that the schooner had run itself aground atop the accumulation of sand near the southeast corner of Tate Hill Pier. The second noise, of course, had been caused by a large section of the top-hamper dropping heavily to the deck.

"There remains one more incident to relate, although I doubt that it is of much use."

"Every scrap of information is of use at this point, Mr. Parker," said Holmes.

"Well, no sooner had the light been trained upon the deck of the beached ship than something that resembled an immense dog leaped up from below and bounded off into the darkness."

Holmes's eyebrows went up at that. "A dog, you say?"

"Yes, sir. I rather fancy that it was a pet of one of the crew members, but I suppose you may have some other theory as regards its presence upon the ship."

"As I have told the good doctor upon more than one occasion, it is a capital mistake to theorise before one has all the evidence. But it seems strange that the captain would allow one of his hands to carry aboard a pet as large as the one you describe, when space is so important."

"Perhaps that question is best left to a student of the Russian mind," commented Parker.

"Perhaps. But we have yet to establish that the captain and crew were as Russian as the schooner."

"Excuse me," I said. "But has no one questioned the members of the crew regarding the mystery of the dead man and the dog?"

"That would be quite impossible, Doctor," replied the journalist, his tone heavy with meaning. "You see, with the exception of the corpse at the wheel, there was no one aboard the ship."

Chapter Two

The Riddle

"Good heavens!" I exclaimed. I looked to Holmes to see if Parker's extraordinary statement had affected him as deeply as it had me, but he retained his languid expression. Presently, however, he sat up in his chair and his face took on all the characteristics of a hunting creature: his complexion darkened, his brows drew together, his lips grew tight. His nostrils appeared to dilate exactly as does a dog's when it is on a scent. It was an expression I had seen him assume innumerable times in his dealings with subjects on both sides of the law, and I hoped for Parker's sake that the account he had given us was accurate, for my friend could be ruthless once he had uncovered a chink in the story of the man he was interviewing.

"Who was first on board the ship after it beached?" he asked the journalist. His voice was strident; there was now no trace of cordiality in his tone.

"The coastguard on duty," answered Parker.

"Did he examine the dead man?"

The visitor nodded. "That was the first thing he examined. Upon receiving his first close-up view of the corpse, he threw up his hands and made an exclamation of terror."

"Indeed! And why was that?"

"Mr. Holmes, I saw the dead man's countenance when I went aboard. It was distorted so grotesquely that it was difficult to believe it was the face of a human being."

"Distorted how?"

"With horror, Mr. Holmes. Naked, unrestrained horror. Such a horror as no man has experienced since the beginning of time, when man-eating creatures ruled the earth."

"You have a poetic turn, Mr. Parker," remarked my friend. "I urge you to put it to constructive use. Describe the body."

Parker's eyes took on a distant appearance, and I could see that he was searching his memory for details. "A man," he said, "some years past middle-age, black-bearded and with skin the colour and texture of old leather. He wore a pea jacket stiff with salt water and a heavy blue pullover underneath. His hands were lashed to the wheel, one over the other in the manner of a seaman who wishes to prevent himself from being carried overboard in rough weather. The chafing of the cords had cut his wrists to the bone. But it was the object he held in the inner hand that most claimed my interest."

"And what was that?"

"A crucifix, sir, with the beads wound around both wrists and the wheel. It was a strange sort of thing to find in those circumstances; hence my interest. That is all I can remember, save for the wounds."

"Wounds!"

"Two puncture marks at the throat, perhaps an inch apart, ragged at the edges and somewhat puckered. The authorities have asked us to withhold that information to avoid panicking the populace with the fear that a wild animal is loose in Whitby. But they were certainly not large enough to have been the cause of the man's death."

"My dear fellow, there are creatures whose bite is scarcely detectable to the human eye, but which is every bit as deadly as a bullet." His eyes slid in my direction. "I would call your attention, Watson, to our earlier conversation concerning Dr. Roylott and the Speckled Band. But this is mere conjecture, and as such it is damaging to the faculties of logic. I assume a physician was summoned?" His eyes transfixed the journalist once again.

Parker nodded. "A surgeon, Mr. J. M. Caffyn, of 33, East Elliot Place in Whitby, was called in to examine the corpse. He declared the sailor to have been dead for at least two days. In the pocket of the man's jacket he found a bottle with a number of pages of closely written script rolled up inside. I caught but a glimpse of them before they were handed to the policeman in charge, but I have since learned that they comprise an addendum to the ship's log. Thus far the press has been refused access to it."

"Excellent!" Holmes exulted, rubbing his hands. "You have a sharp eye, Mr. Parker. And what of the ship's cargo?"

"Fifty wooden boxes, measuring some seven feet by three, containing nothing but plain earth. That information has come to light since my account was filed. I am ignorant as to their ownership or purpose."

"And the dog? Was nothing learned of its fate after leaving the schooner?"

The journalist shook his head sadly. "Alas, that, too, must remain a mystery. If indeed the dog exists, and was not the product of a mass hallucination, it is possible that it has gone into hiding as a result of its ordeal aboard ship. Whatever the case, it has not been reported since."

Holmes sat back, but his cheeks retained the flush which I knew to be a sign of his intense interest in the affair of the moment. "A most appealing problem, Mr. Parker," he said, more to himself than to his guest. "Most appealing."

"Does that mean you will accept the assignment?" The young man looked eager.

"I shall be delighted." The detective got to his feet and extended his hand a second time to Mr. Thomas C. Parker, who rose to accept it. "You may inform your editor that Mr. Sherlock Holmes, who was most impressed with his journalist's manner, will look into the problem, and that he will notify *The Dailygraph* as soon as he has reached a solution. Good day, Mr. Parker, and I wish you a pleasant return journey."

"Well, Watson?" asked my friend after he had seen his young visitor out the door. "What do you make of this case?"

"It seems a most dark and sinister business," I remarked.

"I agree wholeheartedly," he said, with some impatience. "But what of its outstanding points? Have you formed no theory that would fit the disappearance of the crew, the death of the bearded seaman, and the presence of the dog aboard ship?"

I shook my head, frowning. "Only that some of its features put me in mind of the affair of Sir Henry Baskerville of Devonshire and the curse which plagued his family."

"Well, yes, there are some similarities, particularly in the case of the expression of horror upon the dead man's face and of the fleeting glimpse the witnesses received of an immense dog. But do not the tiny punctures in the throat of the captain–I think we can safely refer to him as such, for who else would take such precautions to see that the addendum to the ship's log was not lost–suggest anything to you?"

"Two solutions suggest themselves," I ventured. "One is snake bite–"

He shook his head. "I made mention of the speckled band merely to contradict young Parker's rash statement regarding the supposed harmlessness of such small marks: snakes' fangs do not leave ragged holes."

"–and the other is a poisoned dart."

He smiled. "As in the affair of Jonathan Small and his blowgun-toting aborigine. An admirable comparison, but hardly likely in view of the fact that there were not one but two wounds, with but an inch between them. One dart should have been sufficient; if it were not, I seriously doubt that the victim would present his assailant with a second opportunity, bound though he was. No, our answer lies elsewhere."

"Such as?"

"If you will be so kind as to call upon me tomorrow morning at nine o'clock, I hope to have an answer for you by then. I fear that I will be spending much of the next twenty-four hours sitting in my armchair and poisoning my system with coffee and tobacco as I search through my brain for a solution to this riddle. There's a good fellow."

"Shall I stop in at Bradley's and ask him to send up a pound of shag?" I asked, putting on my hat.

"I have an adequate supply on hand, thank you. Be sure to give my regards to your lovely wife."

I was not in the least offended by my friend's somewhat abrupt invitation to leave him. I knew that absolute seclusion during the long hours of meditation which invariably followed the presentation of an especially knotty problem was as important a tool to him as were the commonplace books he turned to for reference and the concave lens through which he studied the minute clues that helped him solve so many mysteries during his many years of active service. Therefore I did as he had directed, and did not appear again upon his doorstep until the next morning just as the hour of nine was striking.

I found him seated in his favourite armchair, the upper part of his body so thickly veiled in smoke that I would have had difficulty recognising him were it not for the old purple dressing-gown I knew so well. The floor around his feet was a litter of books and loose pages, and I knew without looking that the mantelpiece was all but obscured beneath his drying pipe-dottles from the night before, some of which, as my nose told me immediately upon entering, he was presently engaged in smoking.

"Holmes, the atmosphere in here is intolerable," I said, forgetting for the moment that I was no longer a fellow resident and thus had no right to complain. "I cannot see how the landlady puts up with it."

"I expect that Mrs. Hudson has grown accustomed to my little idiosyncrasies by now, though I should not blame her if some evening I were to return from an investigation to find myself locked out and my bags in the street." He knocked out his pipe upon the table next, to the chair and studied me with an air of detached interest. "You were up earlier than usual this morning, I see."

"I had an early call to make, but how on earth–"

My befuddlement must have shown upon my countenance, for he was moved to laughter.

"Watson," he said, "you would make some talented conjuror an ideal companion. Once he has confided all his little secrets to you, yet would you applaud each new rabbit he plucks from his hat. I know your habits. A man who is as careful about his appearance as you are would never consider donning a pair of stockings that do not match, and yet that is what you have done. It is obvious that you dressed in the dark to avoid waking Mrs. Watson, and that without the benefit of illumination you have put on one black stocking and one grey. That you were up ahead of your wife is also borne out by the fact that she has let you out of the house in such a condition. Am I correct?"

"In every detail," I concurred somewhat ruefully. "It seems so obvious, and yet, until you explain it–"

"The obvious is always difficult. It is that which is hidden that is perceived most readily. No doubt you are wondering what I have been up to in your absence."

"I knew that you would tell me when you thought it right."

"For the most part," said he, "I have been sitting in this chair, poring over the little problem which our journalist friend has placed in our laps and supplementing his information with additional data from the clutter at my feet. Included in the pile are a number of nautical journals, from which I have learned that a sudden shift in the winds at sea, as happened the other night when it looked as if our foreign schooner were about to end its sailing days upon Whitby's infamous reef, is a rare–nay, a nearly unheard-of–occurrence at the height of a shoreward-bound storm."

"Which proves...?"

"Exactly nothing. We can hardly suspect human interference in something as natural as the direction of the wind. But I thought the fact interesting."

"What conclusions *have* you reached?" I inquired, settling myself into the chair opposite and taking out a cigar.

"That it is a case worthy of our interest. But first, what do *you* make of it? Certainly you have evolved some theory since last we spoke."

"I have given it a great deal of thought."

"And?"

"I confess that the waters are too deep for me."

"Come now, Watson. Surely you have formed some conclusion. The disappearance of the crew, for example. What does that suggest?"

"A mutiny, perhaps?"

He shook his head. "If that is what happened, why did they

abandon ship? In such cases it is the captain who is obliged to leave. Certainly no thinking man would turn his back upon a perfectly seaworthy vessel for the black and freezing sea. There can be only one explanation for the crew's absence, and that is that all of them were dead before they left the deck."

I confess that a cold dread came over me upon hearing these words. "Holmes," I said, "are you suggesting that the captain murdered his own crew and cast their bodies overboard?"

"It is a possibility," remarked my friend. "But it is hardly probable. What, then, was the cause of his own death?"

"Heart failure, I should think, brought on by the realisation of the blackness of his deed and by the storm which moved him to lash himself to the helm."

"That does not explain the expression of horror upon the man's face. No, Watson. Whatever killed the crew killed the captain. He saw it coming, he foresaw his fate, and in the instant before death he cried out for help in an area in which there was none to be found and struggled so violently against his bonds that they slashed his wrists to the bone. There was something aboard that ship, Watson, something that no man could look upon without risking the loss of his life or reason. And it is up to us to uncover it."

"What of the dog, and of the strange wounds upon the dead man's throat?"

Sherlock Holmes unfolded himself from his armchair and sprang to his feet in one motion. I could see that one of those sporadic fits of energy about which I have written so much was upon him; his face was flushed and his eyes were like naked blades of steel. "Those, my dear Watson, are the mysteries which you and I are going to clear up when we reach Whitby. Unless, of course, your practice cannot spare you for a few days." He traded his dressing-gown for a jacket and

Inverness and pulled on his ear-flapped travelling cap.

"I am ahead of you this one time, Holmes," said I, exultantly. "I anticipated the invitation and have already seen to it that my patients are referred over to my neighbour. I need merely write my wife a note to inform her that she will not see me for awhile."

"Then write, Watson, write! I warrant that 'The Adventure of the Foreign Schooner' will make an admirable addition to your little collection of thrillers." And with that he was off to hail a cab.

Chapter Three

Sherlock Holmes Investigates

Within the hour we were in a first-class coach and rattling over the rails on the way to Whitby. Holmes would have none of my attempts to draw him into conversation about the case; each time I brought up the subject he turned it aside, with the result that we ended up discussing everything from the opera to the advantages and disadvantages to be gained from having a telephone installed in one's rooms. Not until we drew near enough to our destination to be able to smell the salty air that is the mark of any seacoast town did my companion make any further allusion to the affair of the moment.

"I dispatched a telegram to Mr. Parker this morning to inform him that we would be arriving upon the six o'clock train from London," he said, looking out the window as we slid into the station, "so I should not be surprised if–ah, there is our young friend now."

The journalist was waiting for us when we alighted from the train. With him was an elderly gentleman with long white hair flowing out from beneath the brim of his shining hat and a seamed and wrinkled face that was made to appear even more so by his efforts to keep a pair of gold-rimmed pince-nez perched astride his proud beak of a nose. "I have been out upon an assignment all day, and so did not receive your wire until I returned to the office," Parker informed us after greetings were past. "I was afraid I might miss you."

"Then it is to everyone's good fortune that the train was late. Good day, Mr. Caffyn. I am pleased to make your acquaintance." Holmes favoured the stranger at Parker's side with a cordial smile.

For an instant the other man's face registered shock at the unexpected greeting, but then his eyes flickered down-ward to his black frock coat and he smiled. "You have noticed the bulge of the stethoscope in my pocket," he said, laughing. "For a moment I thought that you had done something remarkable. The pleasure is mine, sir, I assure you."

"Mr. Caffyn has expressed an interest in this baffling puzzle," explained Parker. "I thought that perhaps his findings upon the death of our seaman might prove useful."

"Any information he can supply would be most helpful," Holmes acknowledged, somewhat stiffly. He was smarting over the surgeon's offhand dismissal of his talents of observation.

Parker directed a boy to carry our bags to a four-wheeler he had waiting for us near the edge of the platform, and five minutes later we were clattering along the picturesque streets of Whitby in what I divined from the increasingly strong scent of fish to be the direction of the harbour. "You must be weary after your long journey," the journalist told us. "I have secured a room for you at the hotel. After you have both rested, I should be honoured to accompany you to the schooner."

"I think that I speak for Dr. Watson as well as for myself when I say that we would be most eager to look into your mystery before we rest," replied Holmes, lighting a cigarette.

"I was hoping you would say that." Smiling, Parker directed the driver to proceed to Tate Hill Pier.

"Are there any new developments, Parker?" asked the detective, after we had gone some little way.

"Very little, I fear," was the reply. "But it is a fact that, early this morning, a large half-bred mastiff belonging to an elderly coal merchant near Tate Hill Pier was found dead, its throat torn away and its belly slashed open by a savage claw. I can only gather that this discovery has something to do with our missing canine."

Holmes's eyes shone. "This case gets better and better." He fixed Mr. Caffyn with an interested stare. "I am curious to hear your conclusions regarding the cause of our unfortunate sailor's demise, Doctor," he said.

The surgeon shook his leonine head slowly. "It is a most puzzling case."

"Indeed!" Holmes rubbed his hands. "How so?"

"I can see no reason for it, and yet I would stake my reputation upon the conclusion that the man died of a severe loss of blood."

"And the puzzle?"

"With the exception of the two tiny punctures in the man's throat, which were far too small to be the reason for the loss, there were no wounds to be found upon the body."

I confess that I was shocked almost beyond words by this revelation. My friend, however, retained his air of analytical calm. "Is there anything else," he said, "to which you would draw my attention?"

With trembling hands, Mr. Caffyn removed his eyeglasses and laid them in his lap. His voice dropped to a hoarse whisper, and I was forced to strain to hear his next words. "Mr. Holmes, there was not a drop of spilled blood to be found anywhere upon the ship!"

A dead silence settled over the occupants of the carriage, and for several moments the noise of the wheels grinding over the cobblestones was the only sound. I looked at Holmes and was unnerved by the expression I saw upon his face. He resembled a man who had just seen the principles of a lifetime dashed to pieces. The sight of him like this disturbed me more than anything the doctor had said. When at last Holmes spoke, it was in a grave voice.

"You have my apologies, Mr. Parker," he told the journalist. "Until now I have been referring to your mystery as a little one. I shall not do so again."

An ocean-borne fog had settled over everything by the time we reached Whitby harbour, transforming the rather choppy water into a gunmetal grey and reducing the vessels anchored in the area to indistinct shadows that rocked and swayed with the restless motion of the surface. Near the base of the pier, tilted at such an angle that its severed lines touched the ground, a trim schooner with its sails in rags was perched upon a narrow mound of sand so that only its stern was left floating. One end of the top-hamper lay upon the deck in a tangle of lines and shredded canvas. Enveloped as it was in the choking billows of fog wafting shoreward from beyond the harbour, it looked especially dismal and forbidding, like a ghost ship finally come to ground upon the beach of the Underworld.

A burly coastguard with sagging jowls and red and silver stubble glittering upon his bunched chin pushed up to us as we were alighting from the carriage and declared that the public was barred from the area. When he heard the name "Sherlock Holmes," however, he became suddenly docile and allowed us to pass. "We have you to thank for this, Watson," said Holmes when we had passed out of earshot. "If not for my Boswell, we might have been obliged to resort to bribery in order to gain admittance. Fame has its advantages."

Depressed though I already was by the melancholy business upon which we were engaged, I became even more so as we drew near the marooned vessel. Water slapped hollowly at that portion of the wooden hull which hung over the edge of the sand and the masts groaned beneath the strain of the water-tightened rigging; sending out a most mournful sound. The sight of the beached craft with its blackened prow stabbing skyward and its sails hanging in ribbons reminded me of some awesome sea creature that had become stranded upon land and was crying piteously to return to its home in the ocean's depths. As if that were not enough, the memory of what had occurred aboard this unfortunate vessel within the last forty hours served to underscore my feelings of despair.

"The *Demeter*, gentlemen," intoned Parker, in the manner of a footman announcing the arrival of some important personage at a royal ball. Although he attempted to inject a note of flippancy into his voice, it sounded quite hollow.

Only Holmes, who lived for action, was able to maintain a cheery composure in the face of the ghastly vision which rose before us in the gloom. "The *Demeter*, is it?" he said, approaching the schooner in long, healthy strides. "Ah, yes. Here's the name, all crusted over with sand and salt. The characters, of course, are Cyrillic." Instead of boarding the ship as I'd expected, he spun upon his heel and trudged off across the beach with head bent and hands clasped behind his back, studying the sand at his feet. At intervals he flung himself down onto his stomach and peered at something through his concave lens, then scrambled to his feet again and continued walking in that strange, peering way. While he was following this eccentric course I sneaked a glance at the two men at my side and saw that they were watching him with puzzled smiles. As with most people upon seeing my friend in action for the first time, they did not realise, as I did, that every one of his strange procedures was applied towards a definite end. When at last he returned to where the rest of us were standing, he wore a crestfallen expression which quickly became accusing when he turned it upon Thomas Parker.

"The cargo has been unloaded," he said.

The journalist started as if he had just witnessed a feat of magic. "Why, yes," he said. "Some men came for it this morning with five waggons. I was not here at the time and thus was unable to question them. Their papers were in order, so they were allowed to take away the fifty boxes of earth contained in the hold. But, how–"

"Fools!" cried Holmes, throwing up his hands. "You engage me to solve a mystery, and then you make it impossible for me to do so by allowing others to trample all over the clues and take away the one bit of evidence I need to clear up the problem. Whose side are you on, Mr. Parker?"

Parker was still trying to stammer a reply when Holmes left him and strode towards the gangplank which had been erected upon the ship's starboard side. "Come, Watson," he snapped. "Perhaps between the two of us we will be able to piece together what little remains."

If the exterior of the ship was forbidding, the view from the deck was positively dreadful. It was as if the shades of the slain were still aboard; each shadow took on a weird significance and the creaking of the boards beneath our feet sounded half human, as if we were treading upon the toes of the murdered crew. Around the ship the fog was so thick that we seemed to be adrift upon a phantom sea. I fancied that this was what it must have been like the night the captain scribbled his last fevered entry for his log and bound himself to the helm in the hopes of riding out both the storm and the horror that stalked his ship. I knew better, however, than to confide these somewhat childish impressions to my friend; he would not have heard me anyway, for when Sherlock Holmes was on a case, it was as if the rest of the world ceased to exist. For this reason I contented myself with watching him and remaining out of the way.

He walked the length of the ship twice, head thrust forward, eyes upon the deck. Then he examined the brass rail along the gangway through his glass. Once, I heard him grunt in satisfaction, which meant that he had discovered something; whatever it was, though, it must have been invisible without the aid of the glass, for I could see nothing that seemed worthy of note. Finally he turned his attention to the helm and the rope which hung in loops from the great wooden wheel. I confess that a shudder went through me when my eyes fell to this last. I could not forget young Parker's description of the grisly thing that had occupied that spot only the morning before. But Holmes treated it as if it were the merest bit of bric-a-brac as he ran his glass up and down the woodwork; paying special attention to the bonds, which were spotted in some places with the dead man's blood.

"We are in luck, Watson," said he, returning his instrument to the pocket of his Inverness. "The ignorant fools who allowed priceless bits of evidence to be carted away had the foresight to cut the rope rather than attempt to untie the knots."

"You have reached a conclusion, then?"

"Only that Parker was right in assuming that the captain had lashed himself to the wheel. There are indentations in the rope-ends that could only have been made by the man's teeth as he pulled the knots tight. But at least we know that for certain now. Not that it will prove of any help in determining the identity of the guilty party."

"And your examination of the deck?"

"Yielded nothing. The teak is too clean to show footprints. The rail is a different matter, however."

"May I ask what you found?"

His eyes glinted. "Blood, Watson. Blood. Our friend the doctor was in error in stating that there was none of it to be found aboard the ship. I have discovered no less than three places in which drops of it spattered onto the rail when the bodies of the crew were cast overboard."

My heart grew sick at this fresh proof of the wholesale slaughter that had gone on so near to where we stood. "You are certain that they have been murdered, then?" I asked.

"My dear fellow, I was never in doubt of the fact. But we will discuss these things in greater detail when we get to the hotel. Now if you could see your way clear to rejoin Mr. Caffyn and Mr. Parker while I go below, I shall not be a moment. I imagine that they will be wondering if we have not gone the way of the men of the *Demeter* by now. Be wary of that gangplank when you descend." And before I could concur, he was halfway down the ladder which led to the schooner's dark and gloomy hold.

"You see, Watson," said my friend some thirty minutes later as we shared a bottle of claret in our room at the hotel, "it was imperative to our friend the murderer that every last one of those aboard be killed, for he could ill afford to take the chance of one of them telling what had occurred during that dark voyage. Once the first man had met his death, it became necessary that all of them should end in the same manner."

"But who is he?" I cried. "And why did he kill the first man?" The cheery glow emitted by the little lamp burning on the table between us did little to lift my spirits. The sound of the foghorns in the harbour outside the window bound my thoughts to the death ship, which reposed within a few hundred yards of where we were now sitting.

Holmes's smile was grim, proving that to some extent he shared my mood. "I am afraid I must disappoint you this one time," said he, fingering his wine-glass and gazing into the dark red liquid within. "I have as yet no answer for your first question, and though I have a theory regarding the second, it is too tenuous for me to air it at this time. But I will say this: our murderer is a man of tremendous strength who would experience no difficulty whatsoever in vanquishing the finest professional wrestler that Europe has to offer."

"And your reasoning?"

"Has it not occurred to you that it is no easy task to fling the limp body of a full-grown man over a rail three feet high?"

"Surely it is no feat to drag–"

"No one was dragged."

"My dear Holmes!"

"There were no heel-marks upon the deck and the blood upon the rail was not smeared. No, Watson, our friend the murderer was capable of lifting at least as much as fourteen stone high over his head and hurling it over the side."

"Good lord!" I exclaimed. "If what you say is true, then we are dealing with a brute!"

"Precisely." His voice dropped to a curious guttural, quite unlike the strident tenor to which I was accustomed. "That is precisely what we are dealing with, Watson."

The gravity with which he had delivered this last statement was such that it was a moment before I could gather nerve enough to ask my next question.

"And the dog?"

He opened his mouth and seemed about to answer when he was interrupted by a knock at the door. "Come in," he called.

It was Thomas Parker, but it was a Thomas Parker neither of us knew. His face was pale and glistening, as if he had just received a severe shock, and the fingers with which he held his hat flexed convulsively, wreaking havoc upon the brim of that accessory. His step as he entered the room was uncertain. I wondered if perhaps he were suffering from some sudden malady, and reproached myself inwardly for having left my medical bag in Holmes's rooms in Baker Street.

"My dear fellow!" cried Holmes, rising to help the shaken journalist into a vacant chair. "What has happened? You look quite done in. Watson! A glass of wine for this fellow."

I hastened to do as he asked, but stopped in obedience to a signal from young Parker. "No, it's quite all right," he protested. "It is merely that I am of an excitable temperament, and that the day's activity has proved a bit too much for me on top of my exertions at the searchlight night before last. I will be my normal self again in a moment."

"How may we be of service to you, then?" Holmes asked, assuming his previous seat and reaching for his old brier-root pipe.

"I fear that you will not be pleased by my answer." Parker had gained back some of his colour, but his face was grim. "I am here to ask you to abandon your investigations."

Both of us stared at the journalist, Holmes with a flaming match poised several inches above the bowl of his pipe. He hesitated only an instant, then resumed lighting it. "Indeed?" he said, shaking out the match and depositing it atop the table. "I was not aware that my methods were so unsatisfactory."

"It is not that, sir. The mystery has been cleared up."

My friend's eyebrows went up a bit at that. "I see. May I ask how this has happened?"

The young man reached inside his coat and drew out a black-bound journal which he handed to the detective. "This is a translation from the log of the *Demeter*. All the answers seem to be contained in it."

Holmes flipped through the pages and laid the book before him on the table. "I should prefer to hear your interpretation of its contents, Mr. Parker."

"It seems obvious enough," said he. "The *Demeter* sailed from Varna on July sixth. Aboard were five hands, two mates, a cook, and the captain, who appears to have been the man we found lashed to the wheel. Ten days later, one of the crew, a hand named Petrofsky, turned up missing. A search was launched, but to no avail, and it was decided that he had fallen overboard during his watch. Within a week another man was lost under the same circumstances. By the first week of August, only the captain and his first mate were left aboard ship, all the others having disappeared one by one during the dark hours of the night. The captain himself was manning the wheel at midnight on August third when the mate, screaming incoherently about something horrible in the hold, scrambled up from below and hurled himself over the side. The captain's last entry was written on the evening of August fourth."

Despite the fire which crackled in the fireplace grate, I grew cold as the journalist related these strange and terrible incidents as they were recorded by the *Demeter*'s late master. But Holmes appeared unmoved; if anything, seated as he was in that lazy slouch with his eyes nearly shut and a thick swirl of tobacco-smoke floating about his face, he looked to be half asleep. "An interesting narrative," he commented at last, "but hardly conclusive. You say that the solution is obvious, and yet I confess that the whole affair seems as mysterious as ever to me. Pray tell me what I have missed."

"It is all to be found in these pages," said the other, pushing the sheaf of papers towards my friend. "Did not the captain himself relate in his August third entry that he was convinced his mate, now a hopeless madman, was responsible for the sailors' deaths?"

Holmes picked up the journal and turned to the last page. "Dear me," he remarked after a moment, "he does say that, doesn't he? But what of this entry for the fourth? 'I dared not go below, I dared not leave the helm; so here all night I stayed, and in the dimness of the night I saw it–Him!' And, later: 'But I shall baffle this fiend or monster, for I shall tie my hands to the wheel when my strength begins to fail, and along with them I shall tie that which Held–dare not touch; and then, come good wind or foul, I shall save my soul, and my honour as a captain.' I must say that those are strange words for a man who has seen the perpetrator of these heinous crimes take his own life."

"When that was written, the captain had been at the helm for nearly twenty-four hours without relief. I think we can put it down as the ravings of a man in the throes of complete exhaustion."

"And the captain's death? I am very curious to hear your theory as to what was the cause of his severe loss of blood."

Parker looked embarrassed. "Mr. Caffyn is a fine surgeon," he said hesitantly, "but he is also elderly. I think that perhaps he mistook an anaemic condition for blood loss. The man died, I should guess, of heart failure, brought on by that same exhaustion which caused his delusions."

"My word, but you do have all the answers. Then surely you can explain the presence of the punctures in the man's throat."

"Do not forget the dog," I put in.

"Quite right, Watson," said Holmes maliciously. "By all means, let us not forget the dog."

"The dog, of course, belonged to one of the dead sailors." The journalist was perspiring freely now; I daresay that between the two of us, Holmes and I had quite succeeded in placing our Janus-faced guest in what the Americans call a "hot spot." "I am unable to explain the punctures, unless they were shaving-nicks."

Holmes hurled the journal to the table with a sound like a pistol shot. Both Parker and I jumped at the explosion.

"You, sir, are a fool." The detective shot to his feet and began pacing back and forth between the beds. "What is more, you are a disgrace to the legions of honest men and women who have courted death a thousand times over to make your profession the powerful organ of justice that it is today. To think that the mighty line of Johnson and Shakespeare and Thomas More should terminate in one such as you. Be gone from my sight." He stopped pacing and flung a long thin arm in the direction of the door. "Take your book and leave. My colleague and I have no time for sniveling whelps who grovel before the voice of authority."

All during this tirade I had watched Thomas Parker's face grow more and more pale, and when Holmes was finished, the young man needed no more prodding, for he snatched up his book and his hat and fled out the door almost before Holmes's angry voice had stopped ringing. We listened to his hurried footsteps upon the stairs, followed by the slamming of the door that led to the street, and then Holmes chuckled.

"There is one journalist who will think twice before he places himself in the middle again," he said, re-filling his pipe. But there was bitterness in his tone.

"What was all that about?" I asked.

"The man is covering up, Watson." He struck a match.

"And why should he want to do that?"

"You saw his condition when he came in. Mr. Parker is a very frightened young man. I should think that he has undergone quite a little dressing-down at the hands of his superiors. Someone has decided to lay our mystery to rest."

"Have you any suspicions as to who is responsible?"

He frowned, puffing at his pipe. "It is merely conjecture at this point," he said. "But I suspect that Parliament is involved, and I would be willing to wager that it has something to do with the current animosity in Britain regarding Russia. This growing inclination at Whitehall towards neutrality, I fear, will lead to dire consequences in the not-too-distant future."

"You do not seem surprised at this development," said I.

"I knew that something was in the works when I came upon several sets of waggon ruts leading to and from the stranded schooner, evidence that its cargo had been carried away within the past few hours. You will remember that I said something about it at the time. Paw-prints left by the infamous dog, the chance to inspect the cargo–all have been lost. I cannot conceive of the authorities allowing that to happen unless the action had already received the sanction of someone in the government. I owe you an apology, Watson."

"Whatever for?"

"For embroiling you in a case that can never be solved because of the official ramparts which have doubtless already been flung up in our path. But perhaps I can make it up to you on the way back to London by relating the details of a little problem I solved recently for the Lady Ernestine Carew of Kensington. It had to do with a series of strange messages she received from her late husband through a self-styled spiritualist. 'The Adventure of the Ungrateful Ghost' should offer your loyal readers some entertainment."

I could tell even as he spoke these words that Holmes was bitterly frustrated by the unsatisfactory outcome of the *Demeter* mystery. Had he known what Fate had in store for us, his attitude might have been altogether different.

Chapter Four

The Hampstead Horror

I saw nothing of Sherlock Holmes throughout the remainder of August and beginning of September, although I read of him a great deal. The murder of Sir Oliver Worth-Benton of Coventry and subsequent arrest of his wife occupied the front pages of the London dailies for many a week, and when my friend was able to prove conclusively that Lady Worth-Benton was innocent and that the gardener held more than a passing motive for having done in his employer, one could scarcely walk down to the corner without hearing the detective's name mentioned at least once in the conversations upon the street. As for myself, I was too busy with my practice to leave my consulting room for more than ten minutes at a stretch, for the end of the vacation season had brought back the usual quota of insect bites and summer colds. My mind during these days was so preoccupied with such pragmatic details as prescriptions and diagnoses that I was taken completely by surprise when my wife awakened me from a sound sleep shortly after I had retired on September 27 to inform me that Sherlock Holmes was waiting for me downstairs.

I found him pacing up and down in front of my hearth, muttering to himself and trailing behind him a plume of smoke from his cigarette in the frenzy of impatience he displayed only when the situation was most urgent. He was dressed in his travelling clothes; seeing him thus attired, I was glad that I had taken the time to dress, for I suspected that a journey was in the offing.

"Sorry to knock you up at this hour, Watson," said he. I could see by his flushed cheeks and glittering eyes that he was upon a case. "If Mrs. Watson has no objections, I should like to borrow you for a few days. Something has come up in which your services may prove of no little value."

I looked to my wife with a rueful expression, for she had seen so little of me during the past few days that it seemed inexcusable to compound my crime by chasing off upon some new adventure. I was relieved, therefore, to see that she was not cross with me at all, but that there was an indulgent smile upon her face.

"The vacation will do you good," she said, laughing. "I shall see to it that Jackson takes over your practice. He has been complaining that you have pirated away all of his patients anyway."

"Excellent!" cried Holmes. "Pack a bag, for you will be staying with me until this business is concluded. I have a cab waiting; I shall explain on the way."

"Have you seen a newspaper of late?" he asked when we were both in a hansom and clattering down the gaslit streets of London.

"Not for a few days," I said. I was fully awake now, and eager to hear the details of this latest adventure.

"You will find a summary of the events of the past week on the front page of this issue of the *Westminster Gazette*," he said, placing a thick newspaper in my lap. "I think that one or two of the details may claim your interest."

I turned the paper so as to catch as much as possible of the light afforded by the passing street lamps and looked at it. My attention was immediately arrested by a bold-faced article upon the left-hand side. It was headed THE HAMPSTEAD HORROR, and ran in this way:

> Although there have been no fatalities as yet, the discovery on Hampstead Heath over the preceding four evenings of small children, badly frightened and somewhat weakened but otherwise unharmed except for slight injuries, brings back memories of the shocking atrocities wrought in the East End by the fiend known as Jack the Ripper two years ago. The only information the constables have been able to glean from the young victims, several of whom were reported missing sometime before their discovery, is that a "bloofer lady" dressed all in white had asked them to come with her into the shadows, and that the next thing they remembered was being alone in the darkness until a policeman or an early-morning stroller came upon them and asked them what they were doing abroad at such an hour. In all cases, the tots have shown a uniform lack of ability to explain either their weakness or the wounds found upon their throats. The wounds seem such as might have been inflicted by a rat or some other equally small animal, and their presence suggests that the culprit called the "Bloofer Lady" may be a dangerous monomaniac performing experiments upon small children with laboratory animals, just as the Ripper is believed in some quarters, upon the basis of the apparent expertise of his abominable dissections, to have been a doctor gone wrong.

"What a beastly business!" Shuddering in revulsion, I handed the newspaper back to my companion. The thin swirls of fog outside the hansom had taken on a most sinister significance now that I knew that yet another fiend prowled the shadows of this city of four million.

"Beastly?" Holmes's tone was as if the horrid nature of the situation had not occurred to him. "Well, yes, I suppose you're right. It is of course fortunate that the children have all come out of the business little the worse for wear. But, come, Watson. Surely your professional altruism is not so fully developed that it has been allowed to impair your logic. What significance, for example, do you attach to the children's weakness and the presence of these singular wounds upon their persons?"

I frowned thoughtfully, seeking to imitate as best I could the deductive reasoning of my friend.

"Weakness and dizziness are common reactions to a frightening episode," I ventured. "As for the wounds, it would be foolish in the extreme to blame them upon a chance meeting with a stray animal, since they have shown up on not one but four successive evenings. Therefore, I cannot but concede that the journalist who reported these incidents is correct in surmising that some demented practitioner has been conducting experiments in which a carnivorous beast is set upon a helpless child. The presence of a woman in white would seem to bear out this hypothesis."

"Admirable, Watson!" exclaimed my friend. "I am pleased to note that the years you have spent in observing and chronicling my methods have not been wasted."

I confess to a feeling of pride upon hearing these words, for it was a rare instance in which I was able to elicit a compliment from this extraordinary man. "Then you agree with my conclusion?" I asked.

"No, you were dead wrong."

My mouth dropped open, and I was glad that darkness had flooded the cab in that moment to conceal my dismay.

"I fear, Watson, that in your accounts of my little adventures you have greatly underrated your own part in drawing each case to its successful conclusion. Just as the brightest lantern is useless until it is ignited, the presence of genius without the necessary stimulant that sets it to working is a thing of little worth. Where would I be without you?"

"But, you said–"

"That your theory was incorrect. I did not lie. What possible motive could a scientist, demented or otherwise, have in subjecting stray children to the bite of some predatory creature, then releasing them? Surely this person is aware that wounds will result, and yet the period that elapses between the time these tots are reported missing and the time they are returned to their parents is hardly long enough to observe any further reactions. So your crazed practitioner goes out the window. But take heart, my dear fellow; your function as a conductor of light cannot be overlooked, for you have stated the three most important aspects of this case succinctly and well."

"And they are…?"

He began ticking off the points with his right index finger upon the palm of his left hand. "One. We have a child reported missing. Two. There is a woman in white. Three. The child is discovered in a weakened condition with strange wounds upon its throat. There is, of course, no question that Point Number Two is the connecting factor-between Points One and Three. From them we have no difficulty in constructing a tight little drama involving the abduction and injury of small children by an unknown female. The situation, you see, becomes quite clear once we have formed a narrative to fit the facts."

I shook my head. "I confess that I am still quite in the dark. Why were these children wounded? And what caused the wounds, if not a small animal? These are very deep waters for me."

"As deep, perhaps, as those which closed over the mystery of the missing crew of the *Demeter*?"

Something in the way he said that set me to thinking. I stared at him. "Holmes!" I cried. "You don't think that the two cases are related?"

His smile was grim in the light of a passing street lamp. "Earlier this evening I spoke to the constable who had discovered the latest of the child victims. He described the wounds in the boy's throat as a pair of punctures, roughly an inch apart and torn at the edges. Does this description strike a responsive chord in your memory?"

Once again I saw the helm of the beached ship draped in bloodstained ropes, felt the icy dread that had seized me nearly two months before when I imagined the horrid thing that had recently hung there. "The dog," I muttered, more to myself than to the man riding beside me.

"No, Watson," said Holmes, shaking his head. "Not the dog. That creature, you may remember, was described as immense. The few paw-prints I was able to discern in the sand near the stranded vessel bore out that description. Such a beast's incisors would certainly be more than an inch apart, and hardly capable of inflicting wounds such as those found upon the throats either of the children or of the *Demeter*'s unfortunate captain. The dog–if dog it was–played its part in that affair, but my theory is still too frail to stand exposure. You may recall my observations upon the culprit in the earlier affair."

"You said that he was a man of tremendous strength."

"More than tremendous," he corrected. "I have since learned that one of the men our murderer tossed overboard tipped the scales at sixteen stone. I should not wish to meet the man capable of lifting such a burden in a darkened alley without my stick for protection."

"Do you think that the Bloofer Lady is this murderer, disguised as a woman?"

He laughed mirthlessly. "A strength such as that possessed by our culprit would naturally go hand-in-hand with an impressive size. I hardly think that such a brute could pass himself off as a member of the fair sex."

"But he is involved?"

"Most deeply. But here, I believe, is Hampstead, and there is the infamous heath. Leave your valise in the cab, Watson. I shall instruct the driver to transport it to Baker Street."

As the cab rattled away, we were left alone in the middle of an open tract of land which, although probably quite pleasant during the bright hours of the daytime, appeared most desolate and gloomy beneath the silver shards of illumination cast by a waning moon. Dew glittering upon the well-cropped grass gave it an icy appearance, while all around us evergreen shrubs rose in fantastic shapes and the branches of trees left naked by the first gusts of early winter scratched at the sky like witches' fingers. It seemed the ideal setting for a ghost story, and although my scientific training had destroyed any childish belief I might have entertained in such things as ghouls and goblins, I was sufficiently affected by my surroundings to be glad of the old service revolver which I had had the foresight to drop into my overcoat pocket before starting out.

"No doubt you are wondering what we are doing here in the middle of nowhere," said my friend, in a voice so low that I could scarcely distinguish the words.

"I trust your judgement," said I quietly.

"Good old Watson. I trust that your faith is never shaken."

Admonishing me to be silent, he led the way forward through the shadows. Clouds were scudding before the moon, and at times it was only by following the nearly indiscernible swish of my companion's trouser legs sliding through the wet grass that I was able to keep up with him. At length we came to a halt amidst the shadows cast by a tangle of bushes upon the eastern side of the heath. Here Holmes cupped his hands around his mouth and leaned so close to me that his lips were almost touching my ear.

"From here we command an excellent view of the rest of the heath," he whispered. "I cannot impress upon you too strongly the need for absolute silence."

I nodded to show that I understood.

"You have brought your revolver?"

I nodded again.

"Excellent. I advise you to keep it ready, and to make yourself as comfortable as possible without running the danger of falling asleep. We may have a long vigil ahead of us this night."

I seated myself upon the ground, took out my pistol, and laid it in my lap within easy reach of my hand. Holmes sank into a crouch beside me, his eyes on the moon-drenched clearing beyond the bushes. From where I was sitting I could barely make out his profile against the slightly paler grey of the sky; head erect, torso tilted forward, muscles coiled as if to spring, he reminded me of a crouching lion waiting patiently for its prey to show itself. It was an apt comparison, for what was Sherlock Holmes if not a hunting creature?

The vigil was indeed a long one. I kept track of the hours with the aid of the chimes of a distant tower clock, and yet the time in between dragged by so slowly that it seemed thrice as long. Once in a while I heard the call of a night-bird, now nearby, now far away, but other than that, we waited in silence. I became convinced that nothing was going to happen.

And then I heard a scream that froze the blood in my veins.

"What the devil!" I cried, but Holmes was already off and running in the direction from which the noise had come. I snatched up my revolver and stumbled off in his path.

The scream had sounded from a shadowy section opposite to

where we had been crouching. As we neared the spot, I thought I saw a flutter of something white amidst the blackness, but it was gone so quickly that afterwards I could not be certain that I had seen anything at all. I had little time to think about it in any case, for in the next instant my attention was centred upon the figure which lay motionless in the grass.

It was a small boy.

I knelt to examine him whilst my companion went on in pursuit of the apparition. He returned a few minutes later, seething with anger and frustration.

"She got away. Blast the darkness and blast me for not bringing a lantern! Footprints are of little use when one cannot see them! How is the child?"

"He is very weak," I said.

"His neck, Watson. Are there any marks?"

I turned down the boy's collar, and gasped. In the pale light of the moon, two ragged punctures stood out like plague-sores against the whiteness of his throat.

Chapter Five

A Ghastly Death

I might as well have been alone in the hansom for all the conversation that passed between Holmes and myself during the ride back to Baker Street. The fact that I had been able to clean and dress the boy's wounds and transport him to the charge of a passing constable had done little to lift the detective from the mood of depression into which he had fallen. It was during bleak periods such as this that I feared, most for my friend's health, for though I had succeeded over the years in curing him of the drug habit which had once threatened to destroy that wonderful brain, I knew that the temptation to return to the needle was still there, and that it was greatest when he thought he had failed. He must have sensed my concern, however, because at length he favoured me with a playful slap upon the knee and smiled.

"Don't look so glum, fellow," said he. "My stupidity may have cost us a battle, but the outcome of the war itself remains uncertain. There will be other nights. In the meantime, we shall not waste this opportunity to familiarise ourselves with the problem before we act again. Stop here, driver; I shan't be long."

We had halted before a bookshop, in the window of which the proprietor, either because he had risen early or because he had not yet retired, had left a candle burning. Holmes alighted from the cab and rapped upon the door of the shop with his stick until it was opened, then disappeared inside. When he emerged some minutes later, he was carrying a thick book which he deposited on the seat between us and instructed the driver to proceed.

"It has been most useful to me to learn the names of those merchants throughout the city who suffer from insomnia," he told me when we were on our way once again. "Their misfortune has proven quite the opposite for me, for I seldom have to wait till working hours to lay my hands upon whatever I need."

I picked up the book and glanced at its cover in the faint illumination of dawn. It was leather, and bore the preposterous title *Vampires and Their Brethren from the Time of the Saviour to the Present Day*. The frontispiece was a pen-and-ink drawing depicting a flock of loathsome man-like creatures with great black wings descending upon the prostrate figure of a naked man. Wondering a little about my friend's strange taste in literature at this hour of the morning, I turned to the first page and read the opening paragraph;

What is a vampire (it ran)? He may be a suicide, or one who has sold his soul to the Evil One, or the victim of another vampire. He rests in a casket during the day, and not until the sun descends is he enabled to rise from his grave and stalk the countryside in search of the blood that comprises his unholy diet. He is immortal, yet can he be destroyed. This may be accomplished by seeking him out in his tomb during the hours of daylight, impaling him with a wooden stake driven through his heart, cutting off his head, and stuffing his unclean mouth with garlic. Then only may he who was the Undead rest.

"What drivel!" I cried, slamming the book down on the seat.

"Something wrong, Watson?" Holmes was watching me from beneath heavily drooping lids.

"I am surprised at you, Holmes," said I. "It is an immature mind that turns to superstition merely because a rational explanation is elusive. This is unworthy of you."

His calm was unruffled. "Knowledge of your opponent's qualities, Watson, is a most formidable weapon. I cannot afford to overlook any information which might lead this case to a successful conclusion."

"Have you forgotten what you said at the beginning of the affair at Devonshire? 'In a modest way I have combatted evil, but to take on the Father of Evil himself would, perhaps, be too ambitious a task.' I cannot say that I disagree."

"Then perhaps you have a more down-to-earth theory which will explain the deaths of nine hardy seamen and the appearance of tiny wounds upon the throats of five small children." The detective's voice was sharp. Apparently he did not care to have his own words thrown back at him in this way.

I backed down before my friend's wrath. "I have none," I admitted. "But then I have never pretended to be a detective."

Something in my tone must have tempered him, because he smiled warmly. "Good old Watson. Both feet planted firmly upon the ground, as usual. Once again I must prevail upon you to trust my judgement. Reaching this conclusion has not been an easy process. To do so I have had to abandon nearly every principle I hold dear. I have eliminated the impossible time and again, and always the same improbability remains. If I am wrong, then the blame must rest fully upon my own shoulders."

"And if you are right?"

His face became grave. "In that event, dear fellow, we have a grim task ahead of us. A very grim task."

He fell silent then, and neither of us spoke another word for the remainder of the journey. The sun was slanting in through the windows of Holmes's lodgings when we stepped into the sitting room; only then did I realise how desperately tired I was, for I had had very little sleep within the past twenty-four hours. I left Holmes sitting in his armchair with the vampire look propped up on his bony knees and stumbled off to bed. He was still there when I rose at noon.

"Do you never sleep?" said I, rubbing my freshly shaven chin and blinking like a mole who has been driven from his burrow into the bright sunlight. I sank into the chair opposite him.

Holmes finished the page he was reading and looked up with a smile. "Nothing exhausts me, except inactivity. I have spent a very enlightening morning with my nose buried in this book."

"And?"

"It is a most engrossing work. I have been unable to close it long enough to light my pipe, hence the healthy atmosphere of the room. Did you know that vampires cast no shadow?"

"The subject never came up at the University," I replied.

"It would seem an excellent means of identification. They reflect no image in a mirror, either."

"Anything else?"

"A great deal. It seems that they can transform themselves into a variety of creatures: wolves, bats, moths–to say nothing of dust motes and formless vapour."

I lit a cigar. "Really, Holmes, all this is grotesque. I fail to see–"

He rose, setting aside the book. "Hold that thought, Watson. I don't wish to appear rude, but I must scrape off this disreputable stubble before I show myself upon the street."

"You are going out?" I started to push myself out of my chair, but Holmes stopped me with a gesture.

"Don't trouble yourself," said he. "I anticipate a very dull time of it today, fraught with little of the danger from which I have so often depended upon your courage and ability to rescue me. For your amusement, I recommend the book I have just been reading; if you do not find it suitable, I am certain that you will be able to find something among my bookshelves that will occupy your time until I return."

"I am quite capable of amusing myself in your absence," I remarked, somewhat coldly, I fear.

He smiled. "Yes, of course you are. How stupid of me."

Somewhat ashamed of myself for having rebuked my friend for his kindness, I made an honest effort after he left to make some sense out of the curious volume he had purchased at the insomniac's shop that morning; after finishing the first chapter, however, I grew weary of such things as wolf's-bane and voodoo and screams in the night and asked Mrs. Hudson to send up a belated breakfast. Afterwards I lingered over my coffee as I went over in my mind the points of the singular case upon which Holmes and I were engaged.

I knew Holmes too well to believe that he had gone over wholeheartedly to the supernatural as a solution to the strange events which had led us into the Bloofer Lady's territory the night before. Why, then, did he insist upon playing the part of a wild-eyed spiritualist? I am a person of reasonable intelligence, and yet I confess that my friend's thought processes took place upon a plane so much higher than did my own that I felt a simpleton whenever their result was explained to me without an accompanying explanation of the steps he took to arrive at it. I had been asked to trust his judgement, and trust it I would. This decision made, I chose a volume from among his collection of works on criminal activity throughout history and settled myself in for a pleasant afternoon of reading and smoking.

When Holmes did not return at dusk, I began to wonder if he would be back in time for us to take up our vigil on Hampstead Heath. The longer I thought about it, the more convinced I became that this night would bring misfortune, and possibly death, to yet another innocent child if one of us were not there to prevent it. Thus it was that, two hours after sundown, having seen no indication that my friend would return soon, I threw on my ulster, with the revolver a reassuring weight in the pocket, and struck out for Hampstead alone.

The cab driver expressed some doubt about the wisdom of my getting off at the heath, for it was deserted, but when I paid him he lost no time in quitting the scene. No doubt he was familiar with the details of the Bloofer Lady's crimes and had no intention of becoming her first adult victim. I cannot say that I blamed him, for, now that I was alone in this bleak spot, I began to harbour grave reservations about the advisability of entering into such a business without my quick-thinking partner at my side. But there was no turning back now. Squaring my shoulders, I took a determined step into the darkness beyond the circle of light thrown by the gaslamp upon the corner.

Scarcely had I done so when I heard something which made my blood freeze.

It was a slow, slithering sound at first, as might have been made by some mortally wounded animal dragging itself painfully along the pavement, stopping at intervals to bunch its muscles for its next effort, then pulling itself forward once again. As it drew closer, however, I detected a metallic rolling that reminded me of a piano being pushed down the street upon steel castors. It picked up speed as it neared me, until it was a continuous whirr that could only mean that whatever it was, it had crested the slight rise at the bottom of which I was standing and was coasting down toward me at tremendous speed.

My heart was pounding against my chest. I had thought to bring a lantern with me, but until now I had forgotten it. I whisked off the black cover I had placed over it, and, as the bright yellow beam shone boldly upon the thing that approached me, I slid my revolver from my pocket and prepared to fire.

There was a horrendous screech as the thing came to a halt at my feet. My finger tightened upon the trigger. I braced myself for the explosion.

"Could ye spare a shilling for an old soldier, guv'nor?"

I stared uncomprehendingly down at the speaker. In the frank glow of the lantern, I saw an old man with scraggly grey hair showing beneath a worn cap and a whisky-flushed face peering up at me from the square wooden cart upon which he was seated. The stumps of what had once been legs protruded past the edge of the platform. Above them he held outstretched a horny palm in the manner of a professional beggar. So relieved was I at the sight of him that I fished out a crown and placed it in his hand.

His face lit up at the sight of this unexpected boon. "God bless ye, guv'nor," he babbled, thrusting the coin into the pocket of his shabby coat. "'Tis a decent meal I'll be eatin' tonight, me first in weeks." And with that he placed his palms against the pavement and rolled off into the darkness, leaving me caught between relief and chagrin over my womanish behaviour.

I replaced the cover upon the lantern and left the scene of my embarrassment, stepping into the primaeval wilderness of the heath. It was cold here, and a light mist rolled along the ground so that the trees and shrubs that showed in the moonlight looked as if they were floating a foot above the surface with nothing to anchor them. I had difficulty in finding my way about without my friend's unerring sense of direction to guide me, but after many false turns I at last succeeded in locating the area in which the Hampstead Horror had abandoned its last victim. I knew from my experience with Holmes's investigations that criminals were creatures of habit, and I could see no reason why the "woman in white" would not return to the scene of her earlier crime. With this in mind I concealed myself among the bushes that proliferated in the area and settled down to wait.

I did not wait long. Barely had I sat down in the damp grass when I became conscious of a change in the atmosphere around me. I can define it only as a sudden lowering of the temperature, and yet there was something else, something not of this world, that made me feel distinctly uncomfortable. I felt the hairs on the back of my neck rise. Again I drew my weapon, this time slowly and without noise.

And then I saw it.

My first impression was of a white something, indistinct in shape, flitting through the woods thirty paces to my right. The effect produced upon my consciousness by that sylph-like figure, seeming to float upon the softly curling billows of fog as it flashed in and out among the solid black straightness of the trees, was unearthly. Only, as it drew near did I realise that the figure was that of a woman, and that it was carrying something in its arms. My heart grew sick when I recognised the whimper of a small child. Steeling myself, I rose and stepped out of the bushes, raising my revolver.

"Halt!" The sound of my own voice startled me, so loud was it in contrast to the eerie silence which had preceded it.

At my cry, the woman stopped dead in her tracks and snapped her head in my direction. I gasped involuntarily. I had thought that the years which I had spent with Sherlock Holmes investigating murders of the most vile nature had prepared me for anything, and yet the sight of the face with which I was now confronted filled me with horror and loathing. The woman's hair was golden and her complexion was like silk, but this only served to make the contortion of her features seem all the more ghastly by comparison. Her eyes were wide with hatred, her lips curled back to reveal teeth bared like those of a cornered animal. Like an animal's they were indeed, for the canines were remarkably long and pointed and gleaming white. From her throat issued a sharp hissing sound, much as a cat makes when it believes that its kill is about to be taken away. I recoiled from this naked threat, retreating a step and tightening my hold upon the revolver in my hand.

The change in its expression (I say "it" because I can scarcely reconcile that face, which still haunts my dreams, with that of a human being) when it saw me was astonishing. Immediately the lips closed over those bestial fangs, and the hatred drained from its eyes, to be replaced by a warmth such as I had not experienced since the death of my dear mother. Now I was presented with a lovely visage, feminine in the extreme and marked by cornflower-blue eyes and lips so full and red as to remind me of ripe strawberries glistening with morning dew. The memory of my beloved wife forbids it, and yet I am bound by the demands of truth to record that I was suddenly filled with a hellish desire to be kissed by those lips and to take in my arms the sensuous figure which was only too visible beneath the gossamer material of her white gown. I did not notice when she put down the whimpering burden she had been holding, so entranced was I by the subsequent spreading of her slender arms to enfold me in her embrace. I stepped forward, allowing the revolver in my hand to fall of its own weight to the ground.

"Hold!"

The shout rang harshly in the silence of the heath. The woman in white sprang back, her features contorting once more into a mask of fury. She hissed.

"Back away, unholy fiend!" The one who spoke was a tall man dressed in rags standing behind me. His face was invisible in the shadows, but I vaguely recognised the clothes he was wearing as the same ones which had draped the figure of the legless veteran earlier. At his feet was the little cart, useless now that he was possessed of all his limbs. His voice was brusque, familiar; in my confused state, I was unable to place it. In his outstretched right hand he held something which glittered in the moonlight. At first I assumed it to be a gun or a knife, but on closer inspection I saw that it was a silver crucifix. I decided that I had gone mad.

The hatred in the woman's eyes changed to fear when they fell upon the object in the new-comer's hands. She hissed again, flung her arms before her face, and, with a final sibilant of mixed rage and frustration, turned and fled into the darkness. In another instant she was gone.

I had recovered enough of my faculties to kneel beside the insensate child she had left behind and examine it. Again it was a boy, not more than five or six years old, and very pale from his ordeal. I had peeled down his collar and was inspecting his neck for the familiar wounds when the man who had rescued me from the Bloofer Lady's clutches squatted opposite me.

"Any marks, Watson?"

Now I recognised the voice, as well as the earnest face beneath the threadbare cap, as belonging to my friend Sherlock Holmes.

"None," said I, relieved. "He is beginning to come around."

"We were in time then, thank heaven. And you, dear fellow? You are unharmed as well?" His tone was anxious.

"I am fine. But where is the beggar?"

He grinned, and as he did so, his face took on the shriveled quality which I had marked upon the countenance of the crippled veteran to whom I had given a crown. "Ye mean me, guv'nor?" he croaked, his voice that of the beggar. "Ye'd be surprised what a decent meal can do for a man, even bring back his legs."

I shook my head. Reaction to my narrow, escape had begun to set in, and I was seeking to combat it with a bantering manner. "You have missed your calling, Holmes. The theatre has certainly suffered because of your decision to become a detective."

But Holmes would have none of it. His relief at finding me unharmed had fled, to be replaced by a look of stern disapproval. "You have been very foolish tonight, Watson," he said. "Very foolish indeed."

I did, not argue the point, for at this moment I agreed with him wholeheartedly. Suddenly I remembered the woman. "Holmes!" I cried. "The Bloofer Lady! She is getting away!"

He looked unconcerned. "It matters little, for I know her destination." His eyes flickered past my shoulder. "A constable approaches. We are late-night strollers who have come upon this unfortunate child by accident. Remember that, Watson."

The constable was the suspicious sort; but with some difficulty my friend succeeded in convincing him that we were in fact good Samaritans who had stopped to aid a lost child, and, after agreeing to come down to the station on the morrow to report the incident in detail, we left the boy in the constable's care and struck out across the heath.

"Slowly, Watson," Holmes admonished once we had passed beyond earshot. "He is still watching us. A suspicious action on our part would doubtless land us both in gaol, charged with the Bloofer Lady's atrocities. Constables have no imagination."

By this time my curiosity had quite supplanted my nervousness. Even my guilt over my appalling weakness of a few minutes before had abated in the face of an overpowering desire to know what was happening. "Where are we going, Holmes?" I whispered. "And what bearing has that crucifix upon this case? I am more perplexed than ever."

"Patience, my dear fellow. I promise that before this night is over you shall have all the answers you seek."

For many minutes we continued walking, and with clouds drifting raggedly before the moon it grew so dark at times that I could only tell by the sound of our footsteps whether we were treading upon soft grass or scraping along the well-worn footpaths that criss-crossed the heath. My companion urged me to keep my lantern under cover, lest we give away our movements. At no time, though, did he alter his pace; since it was impossible to detect footprints upon the ground even when the light was at its best, I could only surmise that Holmes was already aware of our destination, as he had indeed announced earlier. Finally we came to a halt before what I perceived to be a fence constructed of steel pikes some six feet in height and linked by means of an ornate scrollwork along the top. At that moment the moon chose to show itself, and a little chill came over me when I saw in its light that we were standing just outside a cemetery.

"The fence is rather higher than it appears in the daytime," said Holmes, breaking his silence of nearly half an hour. "But I think we can manage it, if one of us gives the other a boost."

I suppressed a gasp. "Holmes, you cannot be serious!"

"It is no joke when one middle-aged man asks another to hoist him up over a six-foot-high fence. Of the two of us, my grip is the stronger, so I think our wisest course is to place me on top first, after which I can give you a hand. What say you, Watson? Will the wound you suffered in Afghanistan allow you to support ten stone upon your back for the space of a couple of seconds?"

It was a request, but it was delivered in such a tone that I could do naught but comply. Sighing mightily, I bent down and allowed Holmes to climb onto my back. When he had surmounted the fence, he straddled the scrollwork at the top and reached down a hand. In another moment we were standing inside the enclosure with only the dead as company.

I am not a fanciful man, and yet, standing there among the rows of silent headstones and whispering cypresses, I imagined that I heard in the slight breeze that stirred the grass at our feet the collective moaning of a hundred souls in outrage at this intrusion upon their eternal rest. Tree-boughs creaked ominously as we passed beneath them, and all about me I seemed to sense watchful eyes peering at us out of the darkness. I fingered the revolver in my pocket and was heartened by its cold solidity.

Ahead of us rose a crypt of white marble, its peaked roof and columned façade seeming to glow eerily against a background of fog and darkness. Holmes turned to me, and, placing his finger to his lips, beckoned me forwards in the direction of the grim structure.

"Here is where your lantern will prove useful, Watson," he told me when we were standing before the door of the crypt. "I took the precaution of stashing a similar light in the bushes at the heath, but your appearance has saved me the time I would have lost in fetching it. Pray cast a beam upon the lock and let us see if my talents as a burglar are still–halloa! What's this?"

He had paused in the midst of selecting one of a number of shining instruments from a neat little leather case which he had slid from his pocket to stare at the door. In the light cast by my partially uncovered lantern, it was obvious that the door was already open and that Holmes's burglar kit was unnecessary.

"What can this mean, Holmes?" said I. In my astonishment I

had forgotten to whisper, and my voice echoed in the stillness of the cemetery. This indiscretion brought a harsh sibilant from my companion.

"Draw your revolver, Watson," said he, in a voice so low that I had to read his lips to understand. "There is danger inside." He returned his burglar kit to the inside of his coat.

I did as directed, taking the additional precaution to slip the cover back down upon the lantern, and held my breath as my friend slowly and cautiously pushed open the door. Fortunately, the hinges were not rusted, and it swung inward without a noise. There was a light inside the building. I shielded my eyes against the unexpected glare–and nearly dropped my own lantern when I saw what that illumination revealed.

How can I describe the horror which coursed through my body like an electric shock when I witnessed the scene which unfolded before us in the middle of that dread place? My first impression upon entering was of a group of men crowded around an oblong shape which rested upon a pedestal at the far end of the chamber, like doctors observing a colleague's operation. Unlike doctors, however, they were all dressed in black, with the single exception of the young man in the middle who had removed his overcoat and was standing in that cold mausoleum in his shirtsleeves. None of them appeared to have noticed our entrance, so intent were they upon the task before them. But what a task! After seven years the memory of it is as vivid as it was that night.

The oblong object upon which the strangers' attentions were centred was a casket. Inside, her hands folded upon her breast and her head supported upon a satin pillow, lay the ravishing creature whose charms had so nearly claimed me only a short while before, her eyes closed as if in sleep. At her breast, steadied in the young man's grip, was the charred point of a stout wooden stake some two feet in length. No sooner had these images registered themselves upon my confused mind than there was a swift arc of movement, and a heavy wooden mallet which I had not noticed previously in the man's other hand came down with a crack upon the blunt end of the stake.

The vaulted chamber rang with a shriek of mortal agony. Down plunged the stake, and down and down again as the mallet struck a second and third time. Blood gushed halfway up the javelin in a bright red fountain. The thing in the casket writhed and twisted like a caterpillar pinned to a board, its screams doubling and redoubling in volume, accompanied by the rhythmic pounding of wood upon wood. In the background I was vaguely aware of a monotonous chanting, and that this came from an elderly man standing upon the opposite side of the casket holding a prayer book open in his hands, but my mind was too numb with the horror of the thing to take note of this blasphemy. Abruptly the shrieking halted, and whilst it still echoed around the marble walls I could see that its originator would scream no more.

The shock of the moment was not lost on Holmes. Looking at him, I saw that his face had grown a shade paler and that he had clamped his mouth shut and swallowed hard to keep from vomiting. Nevertheless, his voice was steady when he addressed the perpetrators of this black deed in the silence that had descended like a hundredweight upon the expiration of the thing in the casket.

"Professor Van Helsing, I think?" he said, looking at the man with the prayer book, who reared his head suddenly at the sound of this unexpected greeting. "And these others would be Dr. Seward and Arthur Holmwood, Lord Godalming. The American I do not know." His eyes swept the rest of the gathering, beginning with a sober-faced, black-bearded fellow near the head of the casket and passing across the startled countenances of the blood-bespattered young man and another with blond side-whiskers who wore clothes of a distinctly American cut. Then surprise was plain upon their faces.

It was the American who spoke first. His voice was tinged with an accent that put me in mind of tumbleweeds and vast deserts dotted with cacti. "I'm Quincey Morris, a friend of Lord Godalming," he drawled suspiciously. "Who are you, and how is it you know my friends' names?"

"My name is Sherlock Holmes, and this is my associate, Dr. John Watson. As to the rest, I shall be delighted to trade information with all of you once we have left this place of horror and death."

"I have heard of you." The elderly man's guttural tones also denoted foreign extraction, but this time I recognised a strong, Teutonic flavour. His eyes were hard behind the thick lenses of his spectacles. "Your presence here explains a great many things, particularly why we were able to find the Hampstead Horror in its lair at this hour, when this was to be only dress rehearsal for the real thing tomorrow. I will consider your offer, Mynheer Holmes. But first must I speak with my colleagues."

When the detective nodded, the man called Van Helsing gathered the others together and whispered with them for some moments. My eyes wandered unwillingly back to the thing which a moment before had been a living, breathing woman, and my knees turned to water. I was forced to clutch Holmes's sleeve to support myself. Finally the men separated, and the old professor fixed us both with a penetrating stare.

"Very well," he said, "we will speak. I have a room at the Berkeley. There will we find privacy. There will you tell me your tale and I tell you ours. It is a tale not for the squeamish. It is a tale of Count Dracula."

Chapter Six

The Tale of the Count From Transylvania

"I judge by your friend's expression that he thinks himself in the lair of a murderer," said the professor, once we were all seated in his opulent lodgings in the heart of London. "He has not been told?" He raised his eyebrows in Holmes's direction. This gave his blocky peasant features a comical cast which was quite grotesque under the circumstances.

"He has not been told for the simple reason that I myself did not know until this afternoon," replied the detective.

Seated in an armchair near the door, he had declined the wine our host had offered in favour of his cherry-wood pipe and was at this point busily engaged in filling and lighting it. Upon his knee was balanced the threadbare cap which he had worn in his guise as the disabled veteran. For myself, my stomach was too unsettled by the scarlet scene I had witnessed earlier that evening to accept anything; in any case, I did not drink with killers.

"What, exactly, *do* you know?" The older man's eyes scrutinised Holmes most keenly. In them I saw something of my friend's bloodhound tenacity. I was overcome with the certainty that I was in the presence of two of the mightiest brains in the Empire.

"I know that the woman whose existence you ended so abruptly tonight was a vampire. I know that in life her name was Lucy Westenra, and that she was engaged to be married to young Lord Godalming when she was killed. I know also that the man who condemned her to her undead state arrived in England aboard the Russian schooner *Demeter* which docked under most mysterious circumstances in Whitby on August eighth. I am counting upon you, Professor Abraham Van Helsing, to fill in the blanks."

Astonishment glittered in the other's eyes. His face was broad, the head large above the bushy brows where his reddish hair began, and marked by a strong, straight nose, a wide mouth set in an expression of determination, and a square jaw unencumbered by whiskers of any kind. It was not a particularly expressive countenance, and yet it was plain to me that he was surprised and more than a little amused by my friend's perceptions. At length he broke into a grim smile.

"Your reputation is well deserved," he remarked, nodding ponderously. "It would interest me to know in what manner it is you came to these conclusions."

Holmes finished lighting his pipe and sent a wreath of blue smoke floating towards the ceiling. "There will be time for that later," he said. "In the meanwhile I think that it is in your own best interests to tell us your story now."

"Perhaps." Van Helsing straightened in his seat and glanced at the faces of his friends as if to consult their opinions. I got the impression that this was no more than a formality, that he was in fact firmly in charge and that the decision was entirely his. Nevertheless, he seemed heartened when he received a murmur of agreement in return. Only young Lord Godalming, whose hand had been the one which had destroyed the Bloofer Lady, remained silent, lost in a world of his own. His fingers twisted convulsively about the half-empty wine-glass he held between his palms.

The professor got up from the high-backed armchair in which he had been sitting with none of the noises an elderly man usually makes upon rising, and, hands thrust deep in the pockets of his black woollen trousers, began to wander about the room. His movements, which at first appeared aimless, soon took on a pattern, and as he talked on in his dry, Old World voice I realised that he was constantly checking the door and windows as if he thought that someone may have been eavesdropping. His command of English was good but stilted, and, if I may be forgiven the liberty of omitting some of the many obscurities which dotted his narrative, I shall attempt to set it down much as it was delivered.

"My name, as already you have divined through means which are unknown to me," he began, "is Abraham Van Helsing. I have been physician and lecturer at the University of Amsterdam for many years. There it was that I met Dr. John Seward, and from that meeting evolved friendship which grows stronger with each moment that passes, though he has elected to turn his back upon the diseases of the body to study the labyrinth of the human mind." Here he placed a friendly hand upon the shoulder of the black-bearded man whose facial expression reminded me of that of a professional mourner.

"Knowing his talents as a physician, I was overjoyed to learn that he had left his position as director of the London mental hospital for a time to look into the case of Miss Lucy Westenra, the betrothed of his friend Arthur Holmwood, now Lord Godalming. A robust woman by nature, Miss Lucy had fallen ill early in August, and, in spite of recurrent episodes of seeming recovery, continued to fail until her very life was in danger. Most puzzling to my friend was that each relapse seemed to occur immediately after the lady was discovered walking in her sleep outside her lodgings in Whitby. Then came the incident which, when I learned of it, convinced me that we were dealing with something far more terrible than simple illness.

"Miss Mina Murray, who has since the events I relate married and become Mrs. Jonathan Harker, arrived soon after hearing of her dear friend Lucy's indisposition to help care for her. One night she awoke to find her friend missing, and, when she went out to look for her, saw her sitting upon the stone of a suicide's grave in a cemetery near the house; bending over her, in Miss Mina's own words, was 'something, long and black, bending over the half-reclining white figure.' When Miss Mina cried out, the thing raised its head and turned upon her a white face with gleaming red eyes. By the time she got there, however, it had vanished. Miss Lucy had swooned. Fearing lest she catch cold in nothing but her night-dress, her friend threw a shawl about her shoulders and fastened it with a safety-pin. Later, upon removing the shawl inside the house, she discovered a pair of tiny wounds in Miss Lucy's throat, but she assumed that these had been inflicted by her when she fastened pin. That night her childhood companion took turn for the worse."

"One moment," said Sherlock Holmes. "When was this?"

"The date was August eleventh."

"I see. Pray continue."

"Once again Miss Lucy rallied," resumed the professor, "but soon her health began to fail again and it became apparent that she would die if drastic action were not taken. This is when I was summoned.

"You have been rightly hailed for your powers of deduction, Mynheer Holmes, and yet Van Helsing flatters himself that even your lightning-quick mind could not have arrived at a conclusion faster than did his own once the stricken woman's symptoms were described to him. The thing in the cemetery, the sudden decline, the presence of two tiny wounds upon the throat–*ach!* Was there ever a more classic case of the dark things of the night at work than this? Without hesitation I took the precautions which have been ingrained in me since childhood; strands of flowering garlic I strung about the windows of Miss Lucy's bedroom, a silver crucifix I placed about her neck. Alas, these were wasted efforts, for I had not taken into account the ignorance of Miss Lucy's mother, now lamentably deceased, who the first night of her arrival removed the garlic in order to allow her daughter to breathe the night air. If only that were all that entered the room that night!

"The final decline had begun, and though we were able to prolong the doomed girl's life through blood transfusions–one of which was accomplished through the most opportune arrival of Arthur's good friend Quincey Morris from Texas"–here he inclined his head towards the blond American–"her fate was sealed. Miss Lucy expired on September twentieth. On that night the Bloofer Lady was born."

"What ineffable twaddle!" I could not control myself. I sprang to my feet and confronted the professor, who eyed me with an air of clinical interest. "Holmes, this creature is seeking to escape a charge of murder by claiming that he did nothing more than aid in the destruction of a phantom, when it is obvious that his victim was flesh and blood. I have never seen a more flimsy attempt at disguising one's guilt." I fingered the revolver in my pocket, for a criminal cornered is the most dangerous animal in existence.

My friend remained in his chair, his eyes half-shut behind a veil of tobacco smoke. "Sit down, Watson," said he, in a placating tone. "Your bravery is appreciated, but misplaced. Professor Van Helsing speaks the truth."

I turned to stare at Holmes. My mind was confused; I wondered if perhaps his spectacular brain had become warped through overwork. I sat down, but I maintained my grip upon the weapon in my pocket.

At no time was I more convinced to the loyalty which the physician from Amsterdam inspired in his followers than in the instant before I resumed my seat. Only then did I notice that the other three men in the room had also left their chairs preparatory to wrestling me away from their leader. I knew then what a capital mistake it would be to underestimate the professor.

Sherlock Holmes sat up and let the full force of his penetrating eyes meet the solid imperturbability of Van Helsing's. "How near to Whitby harbour were Miss Westenra's rooms located?" he asked in the clear, clipped tone that reminded me so much of a clever counsel ruthlessly cross-examining a witness.

Van Helsing smiled thinly. "Once again I bow to your remarkable powers of reasoning. From the unfortunate lady's bedroom window one could look out and watch the vessels sailing in and out of the harbour."

"You said that there was a cemetery near the house. What lies beyond?"

"A deserted abbey, very old and in ruins."

Holmes nodded thoughtfully. I noticed that his cheeks were flushed. The expression was not lost upon the professor, who returned the nod, still smiling.

"Then you, too, have seen the connexion," he observed. He was beaming with a childlike eagerness that was not in keeping with the image of the learned man of science.

"I should retire from public life had I not."

"See here," I said, bristling at this meaningless charade. "What connexion are you talking about? I have taken note of everything that has passed between you, and yet I fail to see what these haphazard scraps of information have in common with each other."

Both of them turned surprised faces upon me, giving me the distinct impression that they had forgotten my presence.

"My dear fellow, forgive me," remarked my friend at last. "It is so seldom that I encounter someone with whom I may discuss details without stopping to explain myself that I quite forgot that there are others to whom these points are not so clear. But surely you cannot have missed the significance of the date upon which Miss Murray found her friend swooning in the cemetery?"

"I am afraid that I have," said I, somewhat tersely. I did not relish being called a simpleton, no matter how polite the terms in which the inference was couched.

"Come now, Watson. You who have chronicled so many of my little adventures so thoroughly, albeit sensationally, cannot have failed to note that Miss Westenra's victimisation occurred less than three days after the *Demeter* ran aground in nearby Whitby harbour."

"Good heavens!"

"By the same token, it should not surprise you to learn that the cemetery lies between the deceased woman's lodgings and an empty house that would be an ideal hiding place for the murderer of a shipload of sailors."

I struck my forehead with the heel of my right hand. "Great Caesar, I *am* a simpleton!" I cried.

"Not at all. You have had a very rough time of it this night; it is no wonder that your perceptions are dulled, as are indeed my own, or you would not have come so near to losing your life in the heath because of my tardiness." He swung his attention back to the professor. "You mentioned a name earlier this evening that was unfamiliar to me. Who is Count Dracula?"

A sly expression came over Van Helsing's countenance. "We struck a bargain, Mynheer Holmes," he said. "First I must hear how you have come to know what you know."

Holmes made a gesture of impatience. "That is of little consequence. I pride myself upon my ability to trace footprints, and have even published a little monograph upon the subject. This afternoon I returned to the heath and followed the impressions left by the Bloofer Lady's quite tangible feet to the Godalming crypt. After that it was a simple matter to peruse the back issues of the local Hampstead newspaper in the library until I came upon the death notice of one Miss Lucy Westenra, betrothed to Lord Godalming and attended during her illness by Dr. John Seward and Professor Abraham Van Helsing. When I learned that she had been transferred here from Whitby, my interest became acute. Lest my appearance abroad on such a night draw too much attention, I obtained from a reformed cracksman of my acquaintance the material for what I flatter myself was an ingenious disguise; I was wearing it when I made contact with Dr. Watson. It did not seem going too far afield to identify the men we found gathered around the casket this evening as those mentioned in the newspaper. I believe it is your move, Professor."

"Brilliant!" Van Helsing exclaimed.

"But very elementary," responded my friend.

"It is the very simplicity of the thing that I find so brilliant. But I have paid you compliments enough for one night." The professor removed his spectacles and began wiping the lenses with his handkerchief. The eyes thus exposed were like two flat discs of dull steel, hard and immovable. "Who is Count Dracula," he intoned, frowning. "As well may you ask me who is Lucifer, for the two have much in common. Perhaps I should begin by telling you who *was* Count Dracula, and by this means prepare you for the odds we face in dealing with who he is." He replaced his spectacles. Behind them, his eyes took on a glitter that was every bit as intimidating as that which appeared in my friend's eyes when he was probing a subject's testimony.

"According to my friend Professor Arminius of the University of Buda-Pesth, Dracula was that proud descendant of Attila's who led his horde against the blood-thirsty Turk over four centuries ago, and who in his deeds surpassed even the gory excesses of the Sultan's own. Even then, in the days before it is said he offered his immortal soul to the Evil One in return for everlasting life, Dracula was spoken of as *wampyr* and *berserker* by his followers as well as by his enemies. Still is he spoken of as such, for in the land which once he ruled, superstition holds reign as surely as does your good Queen in these enlightened isles. It is at this point that our interest begins.

"I have mentioned the name Jonathan Harker, but I have not yet explained his connexion in this affair. He it was who, in May of this year, journeyed to Castle Dracula in distant Transylvania to aid the Count as solicitor in purchasing a suitable dwelling near London. This much I know from what his wife, the former Mina Murray, has told me. I hope to learn its whereabouts later, for I have this night received telegram from that wonderful lady informing me of her arrival in London by train at six o'clock tomorrow morning. It is only recently that we have learned we are working on same case; hence our failure to compare notes. I do know that Mynheer Harker's stay in Transylvania was a circus of horrors from which he was able to escape only through terrible risk of his life.

"What took place after this unknown estate was acquired by Dracula I have been able to piece together from newspapers and from my own experience. The appearance in Whitby of Russian schooner piloted by a dead man last month, carrying a cargo of fifty boxes of earth, tells me that Dracula has docked in England. He it was who condemned our poor Miss Lucy to her undead state, from which we were able to free her only this evening. The ruined abbey next to cemetery in which she was first attacked provided shelter for the Count until he could travel to London. As Miss Lucy's avengers, our next step is to, seek him out in his present lair and destroy him before he can contaminate another soul."

My face must have betrayed my disbelief, for Van Helsing fell silent and directed the full force of his gaze upon me.

"I see, Doctor, that you are sceptical." His voice was drily accusing.

"I most certainly am!" said I. "I am astounded that you; a man of science, should fabricate such an outlandish fairy tale in order to mask your own part in this grisly affair. You must think us fools."

"On the contrary, Doctor. If I thought this, you can be assured that I would not have told you what I have already. There is a realm in which dark things lurk, a realm which has no boundaries, so that these dark things are free to weave themselves in and out of the tapestry of the life we know. Among these are vampires.

"I once laughed, as do you, at idea of corpses that prey upon the blood of the living. I laugh no more, for I have seen the evidence of their unholy existence. Now I know their strengths and weaknesses as well as I know my own. By day are they powerless; then must they rest in caskets upon or beneath the soil of their homeland. Until now, we who have studied *nosferatu*–the Undead–believed that this of necessity bound the vampire to his native shores. We were wrong. This Dracula, he is crafty. By taking with him ample supply of earth from Transylvania, he is free to haunt the four corners of the globe with impunity so long as he may remain undetected. We know of his appetite; the deaths of nine seamen during month-long voyage from Varna to Whitby has told us this. We know from appearance of what observers called 'immense dog' on board of beached ship that Dracula can change his shape at will. Had I been there at the time, I would have identified the creature as a wolf, for these are much more common than dogs in the wilds of Transylvania. My studies add that he and his brethren can assume also the outward appearance of bat, moth, rat, owl–aye, even dust motes and vapour–whatever prowls at night. He can, at least in his immediate vicinity, command the fog, the wind, and the storm. We have seen this last power manifest itself in sudden gale which struck Whitby on the night of the *Demeter*'s arrival. Miss Lucy's rebirth as Bloofer Lady is evidence enough that his victims become themselves vampires. As if all these things are not enough, he has the strength in him of two dozen men, for who but a brute could have succeeded in hurling overboard the limp corpses of his victims at sea?" He raised his eyes from mine and swept them about the room. "So now you see, gentlemen, the magnitude of the task we have set for ourselves."

"But what of his weaknesses?" It was Lord Godalming who spoke. His colour had returned, but his eyes were feverish with hatred for the thing that had taken his bride-to-be. The glass in his hand was empty. "Have we no weapons with which to combat this fiend?"

"Weapons we have aplenty," replied Van Helsing calmly. "Wolf's-bane is one, garlic another. These things the vampire avoids. Most feared is the Holy Cross and all that goes with it. By day and by night may we operate, while during the hours of sunlight must Dracula rest. Running water he cannot cross. And, to bring to an end his unclean existence, we have the wooden shaft. By such means may the vampire be rooted out and destroyed like the malignant growth he is."

"Bravo, Professor Van Helsing!" Holmes was up and out of his chair with the speed of a striking cobra, his lean body crackling with energy. "You have laid out a preliminary plan of action much as I would have done myself. The information with which you have provided us is of great value. In return, my colleague and I would be happy to lend our own limited powers to the task you have so eloquently described."

Van Helsing turned an impassive face upon the detective, "I am grateful, Mynheer Holmes, but that will not be necessary."

It was not in my friend's manner to show surprise, and yet I detected a faint glimmer of astonishment in his eyes upon hearing these unexpected words.

"Please do not take offence," the professor went on. "It is not that we would not welcome the application of your remarkable powers to this labour, but rather that we would prefer to avoid notoriety." He glanced at me. "Even in my country we are familiar with the good doctor's accounts of your more interesting cases, and I think that I speak for my companions as well as for myself when I add that we are anxious not to have publicity that may panic all of Britain. Dracula must pass from this world enshrouded in the same secrecy in which he entered it."

"I assure you, sir," said Holmes coldly, "that Dr. Watson and I will be most discreet."

"I am sorry. I must ask you to leave so that I may confer with my companions."

"Why, if you do not desire our assistance, have you told us so much about Dracula? Why didn't you simply refuse to take us into your confidence?"

Van Helsing looked amused. "Suppose I had," he said. "Would you have abandoned your investigation?"

"Certainly not."

"There. You see?" He turned away. Holmes took hold of his arm and spun him around. The other men in the room sprang to their feet in the same instant, only to stop at a signal from the man from Amsterdam. They stood poised to defend him.

"You are committing a grave error, Professor Van Helsing. I urge you to reconsider."

The professor's eyes grew hard. "The matter is closed. If either of you should attempt to interfere, I shall be forced to see that you are arrested for invasion of privacy. Lord Godalming has powerful friends in Parliament. Good day."

"Come, Watson," said Holmes, turning on his heel.

"Well, I suppose that's that," I said when we were seated in a hansom a few minutes later on the way back to Baker Street.

"On the contrary, Watson," remarked my friend, puffing on his pipe. "*That* is definitely not what it is."

"Whatever do you mean? I can see us going no further on this business without Van Helsing's aid."

"Perhaps you're right." He smiled mischievously. "I wonder which train Mina Harker is arriving upon tomorrow morning?"

Chapter Seven

We Meet the Fiend

I awoke before dawn the next morning to see a light glowing in the sitting room. Putting on my dressing-gown and slippers, I went down and found Holmes seated at his desk poring over the train schedules in Bradshaw's.

"Holmes," said I, "you are courting disaster. Even detectives must sleep from time to time."

He smiled, putting away the book. "You are quite right, dear fellow. Which is why I caught an hour's sleep upon the divan before applying myself to the puzzle of deciphering the nineteenth-century's answer to the palimpsest."

"And what have you discovered?" I took a chair next to the fireplace, for it was a cold September morning.

"That the only train arriving in London at six o'clock this morning is an express from Exeter. This, no doubt, is the conveyance upon which Mrs. Harker is steaming to Paddington at this very moment."

"We are going to meet it?"

"We will meet it, but not at Paddington. I have discarded my customary frugality long enough to hire a four-wheeler with a very capable driver who assures me that he can deposit us at said train ten miles before it reaches the city. That will give us time to speak with Mrs. Harker before she falls beneath the influence of her stubborn friends."

"But how are we to board it? You said yourself that it is an express."

Holmes's smile became mysterious. "Tell me, Watson," said he. "What sort of runner were you when you played Rugby for Blackheath?"

"Good lord!" I half-rose.

He chuckled. "Steady, Watson, steady. There is a jog in the tracks ten miles southwest of London for which the engineer is obliged to slow down. I should think that even a pair of middle-aged city-dwellers such as ourselves will find little difficulty in boarding a train that is rolling no faster than fifteen miles an hour."

"Arid if the conductor should not approve?"

"The price of two tickets, together with an extra half-sovereign which the railroad need never know about, will, I am sure, solve that problem. The worst that can happen to us is that we may be thrown off. In that possibility lies the danger and the charm of the thing. How about it, Watson? Are you game?"

"I have braved poisoned darts and the fangs of a maddened hound at your request," I informed him. "I see no reason why I should quail now, when the most I have to fear is a few bruises. My pride has been tested before, and it inmost impregnable. Yes, I am game."

"There's the Dr. Watson I know. Very well, then, put on some clothes. We have a train to catch, and for once I am using that term in its full literal sense."

The sum which Sherlock Holmes paid for the use of the vehicle and its driver must have been lordly, so numerous were the chances we took during the harrowing journey through the streets of London and across the open country beyond. The shrill screams of policemen's whistles and the shouted curses of other drivers with whom we had nearly collided were still ringing in my ears when we left the city behind us and raced along the twisting unpaved roads that led to our destination. The carriage rocked from side to side over the rutted paths with the violence of a ship caught in a typhoon. Only Holmes seemed oblivious to the risks we were taking; sitting beside me with his hands braced against the seat and side of the conveyance, head thrust forward so that the cords of his neck stood out like taut lengths of twine, his profile was that of a foxhound close on the trail of its fleeing quarry. As for myself, I could only hold on for dear life and be grateful for the fact that I had not broken my fast that morning, for my stomach was anything but steady.

When at last we came to a stop in the centre of a dense cloud of dust, we were within a hundred yards of the railroad tracks, which, true to my friend's words, described a lazy semicircle around a grassy mound of a hill before straightening out and disappearing into the horizon. Holmes was out of the carriage before it stopped rolling. I waited until the dust had settled and joined him a moment later.

"We are not an instant too soon," he remarked, pointing westward, where a plume of dirty grey smoke showed clearly against the pale sky. He fished a coin out of an inside pocket and handed it up to the driver. "An extra sovereign for a job done admirably. Back to town with you, cabbie, and mind the speed limits on your way in."

The driver tipped his hat, then turned the horses around and departed at a stately pace. The chugging of the locomotive was audible now in the distance, punctuated at intervals by the strident squeal of its whistle as it approached a series of level crossings.

"Our trial is near at hand," observed my companion. "Are you ready, Watson?"

"As ready as I will ever be," said I.

"Be of stout heart. I am told that the American bandit Jesse James made a career out of doing precisely what we are about to attempt."

"I seem to recall that he was none too successful in the end, however."

"A wholly unrelated incident. He was shot in the back, I believe, by his cousin. The wages of sin is death."

"You certainly have a way of heartening a fellow," I muttered.

Holmes chuckled.

The train was a moving black bar, overhung with a spreading dark fan of smoke. I could feel the vibration of its approach beneath my feet. Once again the whistle sounded, by now so close that I jumped at the noise. I looked at Holmes. He retained his outward calm, and it was only by observing the rapid dilation of his nostrils that I, who knew so well his many idiosyncrasies, was able to gauge the extent of his excitement. It was for moments like this that my friend lived.

"It's slowing, Watson. Get ready."

The chugging diminished as the train neared the bend, broken by the intermittent hissing of its brakes being applied, and with a gentle rumble the locomotive and its burden began the long slide around the hill. I squinted against the dust that flew up from the cinderbed and waited for the signal to act.

"Now, Watson! Grab hold!"

Even as he spoke, Holmes grasped the steel handles at the rear of the guard's van and swung himself onto the steps that led to the back entrance. The wind caught his Inverness and sent the cape billowing out behind him. I hesitated an instant too long, and had to run to catch up. The train was beginning to pick up speed. I lunged for the railing, purchased a grip, and with the help of Holmes's grasp upon my right wrist, pulled myself aboard just as the train left the bend and charged into the straightaway.

"That was rather close," said I, looking down at the ground, now no more than a blur.

"Too close, dear fellow." There was relief in the detective's voice. "It's a long, walk back to London."

The guard, a large-boned old man with a walrus moustache that bobbed and bounced when he spoke, threatened to throw us off the train, but Holmes had been right when he surmised that gold would smooth his ruffled feathers. Once a sovereign had changed hands we had no difficulty in learning from him the location of Mrs. Harker's compartment; he insisted, in fact, upon escorting us there personally.

"Mrs. Harker?" asked Holmes of the daintily attired woman seated alone in the compartment as I closed the door behind us. He had removed his cap and was holding it in one hand.

"You have the advantage of me, sir." She showed neither surprise nor consternation at our presence uninvited in her compartment. If anything, the lovely, sweet-featured face which was turned upward towards us beneath the broad brim of a flowered travelling hat appeared inquisitive, as if she, too, were searching for information. To use Holmes's own words from another occasion, this was a woman with a mind.

"My name is Sherlock Holmes and this is my friend and confidant, Dr. Watson; Forgive the intrusion, but we wish to ask you a number of important questions which may help us solve an unpleasant mystery."

"Has this anything to do with Count Dracula?"

Holmes eyed her approvingly. "You know then," he said.

She smiled, a sweet, feminine smile. "Not everything. Not yet.

Please sit down. I have heard of both of you, and I am willing to co-operate in any way that I can if it will aid in bringing to a close the career of the fiend who nearly drove my husband out of his mind."

He thanked her and we took the seat opposite. "That is the first thing I would like to ask about," said Holmes. "What can you tell me of Jonathan Harker's stay in Castle Dracula?"

"I can tell you nothing but what I have learned from reading my husband's journal," said she. "I am afraid that you may put his entries down as the ravings of a hopeless lunatic."

"Very little would surprise us at this point. Please begin."

"As a solicitor, Jonathan was invited to go to Transylvania to draw up the papers by which Dracula intended to purchase an estate in England," commenced the lady. "On his way to the castle he encountered a number of superstitious peasants who urged him to turn back, but he ignored them. He found Dracula a genial though slightly sinister host who looked forward to an enjoyable stay in England. The terms specified in the contracts met no resistance from the Count; within a very short time Jonathan's work was completed and he made plans to return home where we were to be married soon after. His host, however, appeared reluctant to let him go and insisted upon having his guest remain in Transylvania for at least a month. Jonathan's protests fell upon deaf ears.

"It was not long before my husband discovered that he was a prisoner in Castle Dracula. The fact that there were no mirrors anywhere upon the premises and that his host never appeared during the daytime had aroused his suspicions, and one day, exploring the castle in search of an answer to his many questions, he found all the doors leading to the castle's exits locked tight. That evening he received the shock of his life." Here she paused and seemed reluctant to continue. Holmes looked at her sympathetically.

"There is no need for embarrassment," he told her. "After what we have seen we are prepared to believe anything. What was the nature of the shock?"

She nodded and went on. "In a beam of moonlight outside one of the windows in the corridor, he saw Dracula, head down, his cloak spreading behind him like the wings of a monstrous bat, crawling *straight down the castle wall in the direction of the courtyard.*"

"Good heavens!" I exclaimed.

"There is more, Doctor," she said. "Astounded though he was by this chilling sight, it was not until the next day that Jonathan learned the awful truth about his keeper.

"My husband is a brave man, Mr. Holmes. He decided that if Count Dracula could climb down the wall, he could too, and with the aid of a trellis he descended into the walled courtyard, at the rear of which stood a small chapel. Inside he found Dracula lying in a death-like trance within a casket which bore his coat of arms upon the lid. His face was bloated and his lips were smeared with fresh blood. Jonathan flew into a rage at the sight of this loathsome leech; picking up a nearby shovel, he determined to deal a death-blow to the thing, but at the last instant Dracula opened his eyes and threw off Jonathan's aim so that he did no more than open an ugly gash in the fiend's forehead. Knowing now that the Count would never allow him to leave the castle alive, for that would endanger his plans to conquer England, Jonathan scrambled over the wall of the courtyard and ran for his very life.

"So great were the horrors he had experienced while under the monster's roof that he went out of his head for a time, and for many weeks he lay screaming and babbling in a Buda-Pesth sanitorium until his doctors were able to get in touch with me and ask me to join him. It is there that we were married. We thought then that the nightmare was over; we were wrong. Jonathan had only just recovered from his ordeal when Professor Van Helsing informed us that Dracula was in England. That day my husband pledged himself to destroy his former tormentor. At present Jonathan is in Whitby, attempting to track down the fifty boxes of earth with which the Count landed last month."

The remarkable tale which the lady told, together with the calm, emotionless manner in which she described those horrors which had nearly cost her husband his sanity, had engrossed me to the extent that for a long moment afterwards I was left in the wilds of far-off Transylvania, where jagged mountains loomed black against the sky and wolves howled in the wilderness. It came as a shock when the train whistle sounded and reminded me that I was in fact seated in a safe compartment speeding through the picturesque English countryside on the way to London.

I admired Mrs. Harker's cameo-like profile against the window and felt a new respect for this lady who had not shrunk from the prospect of hauling the man she loved back from the brink of madness. Nor was I alone in this sentiment, for it was in a tone of deep reverence that my companion spoke to her after a pause of nearly a minute.

"The bravery of your husband is equalled only by your own, madam. One question remains. Did Harker confide to you the name of the estate he procured for Count Dracula?"

"He has done better than that, Mr. Holmes," said the lady. "He has provided me with photographs." So saying, she reached into the carpet-bag on the seat beside her and drew out a tissue-wrapped parcel which she unwrapped and handed to the detective.

The photographs depicted a rambling structure of ancient stone resembling a castle keep and surrounded by a high stone wall, the iron gates of which were encrusted with rust. Its run-down appearance was heightened by the numerous trees which grew within the enclosure and gave it an air of permanent gloom. Although mediaeval in architecture, parts of the structure appeared to be newer than others, numerous additions having been built over the centuries until the interior must by now have been a veritable labyrinth. I could almost smell the fustiness which surely hung about the moss-covered masonry.

"It is called Carfax, and it stands upon a by-road at Purfleet," Mina Harker informed us. "My husband took these photographs with his Kodak before leaving for Transylvania where he intended to show them to Dracula. It covers some twenty acres and is surrounded by only a few houses, one of which currently shelters Dr. John Seward's lunatic asylum. I do not imagine you have met the good doctor? He is connected in a most unselfish and dedicated manner with a tragedy which recently befell my dearest friend in this world."

"Yes, we are familiar with the sad case of Lucy Westenra," said Holmes, returning the photographs.

She raised her eyebrows at that. "Indeed? I did not know that there was any connexion between poor Lucy's death and this sordid business."

"It is not my place to say anything more. But here, I believe, is Paddington." He rose. "Good day, Mrs. Harker. Your testimony has been most informative. For reasons which must remain my own, I must request that you speak to no one about our visit. Come along, Watson."

We waited until Mrs. Harker had departed with Dr. Seward, who had come to meet her, before leaving the train. Holmes was in an unusually exuberant mood as we left the station and fell into step with the strollers upon the street, whistling passages from an opera, which I could not identify, in time with the swinging of his stick.

"Well, Watson?" he said at last. "What do you think now?"

"That Mina Harker is a woman with a remarkably strong constitution."

"That is as undeniable as it is obvious. But I was speaking of the case. You are still sceptical?"

"I am always sceptical," said I. "But I admit that I am not as sure of my ground as I was. It would be pushing the law of averages too far to suggest that everyone we have spoken to in connexion with this case is suffering from the same delusions."

"It would be a most amazing coincidence," agreed my friend.

"At the same time, all my scientific training rebels against the notion of Supernatural beings that rise from their graves at night to feed upon the blood of the living and command fog and storms to cover their tracks."

He nodded. "It does seem a small world to contain two such divergent modes of thought. Perhaps we shall be able to reconcile them tonight, when we journey to Purfleet and pay a call upon the vampire in his lair."

Nothing more was said about the undertaking until that night. Holmes spent the remainder of the day at his acidstained laboratory table conducting a series of increasingly malodorous experiments with the chemicals he kept upon a shelf in the corner while I pored over a stack of new medical journals which I had brought over from my house. At dusk he rose from his place across the dinner table from me, and, after exchanging his dressing gown for a jacket and ulster, drew a revolver from the drawer of his desk and dropped it into his pocket. He saw me watching him curiously and smiled.

"I am quite aware that Van Helsing did not include bullets among those weapons he considers effective against this singular foe," he assured me. "But one never knows what tangible horrors he may encounter along the way, and hot lead has never failed me as a recourse against London's more conventional villains. I would suggest that you bring your pistol along as well."

It was not quite dark when we stood before the rusted iron gates which I recognised from Mrs. Harker's photographs as the entrance to Carfax Estate. Even so, the dense growth of trees inside the wall blotted out what little light remained so that beyond the gates it was black as sable. Somewhere a shutter was loose and it banged incessantly in the wind, creaking upon ancient hinges. It seemed a perfect setting for one of those trashy horror stories which at that time glutted the book-stalls. At Holmes's request I lifted the lantern I was carrying so that its light shone upon the huge iron lock; selecting a skeleton key from among the many on the ring he had taken from his burglar's kit, he inserted it and, in no more time than it takes to unlock a door with its proper key, sprang the tumblers and eased open the gate. It creaked alarmingly.

"That's done it, I'm afraid," said Holmes. "Well, there was no other way. Step carefully, Watson; he knows we are here now."

The walk from the gate to the front door was lengthy, and the trees grew so close together that in places we had to continue in single file. The silence, save for the irregular banging and squeaking of the invisible shutter, was overpowering. For the second night in a row I felt as if I were being watched. This feeling increased as we drew near the building, until by the time we were standing before the iron-banded oaken door I was obsessed with the certainty that our every move was under the scrutiny of unseen eyes.

Holmes succeeded in unlocking the door with the second key he tried; and with an effort, for the door was thick and heavy, we pushed it open and stepped inside. The first thing my light fell upon was an enormous spider's web which spanned the entire entrance-way; its strands were thick with dust and appeared strong enough to trap a small bird.

"There is something wrong here, Holmes," I whispered. "It is quite evident that no one has been here for a very long time, else he would have parted this web upon entering."

"We are not dealing with an ordinary man, Watson. Besides, there are other entrances."

With his stick Holmes cut through the web and led the way into the lofty main hall. Immediately my nostrils were assailed by an odour so foul that my first impulse was to hold my breath against it. It was not the stale smell one expected of a building that had been closed up a long time, but was rather the all-pervading stench of evil. Perhaps the terrible purpose which had led us here had caused my imagination to work overtime, but I could not escape the feeling that wickedness hung about this place as surely as the tattered banners of ancient cobwebs which dangled in the corners and the thick layer of dust which lay like a carpet upon the sunken floor. Once my companion stopped and directed me to shine my light upon the floor at his feet. I did so, and suppressed a gasp when the clear outline of a man's boot-print sprang into view against the grey dust.

"Hobnails," said Holmes. "The unmistakable sign of the British workman. You see, Watson, there *are* other entrances."

How long we spent wandering through that ancient maze I cannot guess, but when we at last descended a short flight of steps to the low, arched door of the chapel, my lungs had grown accustomed to the choking atmosphere of the place as if they had never tasted fresh air. Nevertheless, I was completely unprepared for the fresh wave of foulness which was belched into my face when the door was opened. So vile was this mixture of blood and corruption that the air

I had been breathing since entering the building seemed sweet by comparison. My stomach lurched against this miasma of death, but I steeled myself and stepped forward into its midst upon the heels of my companion. It grew stronger the farther we advanced. We were in the exact centre of the room, where the stench was worst, when we saw the boxes.

Some were stacked in corners, but for the most part they were scattered all around the room. They were between seven and eight feet long and a yard in width, and those whose lids had been removed were filled almost to the top with black dirt. At Holmes's direction I raised the lantern as high as I could while he counted them. When he had finished he turned to me, and in the eerie yellow glow cast by the oil flame his face was grim as death itself.

"There are only twenty-nine boxes," he said.

"Are you quite certain?" I asked after a pause.

"I have counted them twice. There are none in any of the other rooms we have been in, and I believe we have visited all of them. I can only conclude–" He fell silent suddenly, and when I opened my mouth to inquire what was the matter, he silenced me with a gesture. His attention seemed to be centred upon something beyond my right shoulder. Slowly I turned to see what it was.

In the instant of turning I received the impression that someone was standing in the darkened passage beyond the chapel's arched doorway; indistinctly I made out what appeared to be the highlights of a face, of a high forehead and an arched nose and a square chin awash in inky blackness. By the time I had finished turning; however, it was gone, leaving me uncertain that it had been there at all.

Holmes was moving by this time. Drawing out his revolver, he crossed the room in three strides and stepped cautiously into the passage. Almost immediately he drew back. I stepped forward to aid him–and stopped in horror when I saw the reason for his retreat.

At first I was aware only of a phosphorescence, of hundreds of tiny red lights which twinkled like gems in the darkness. As they came forward, I saw them for what they were, and my hand went instinctively for my own revolver. They were the glowing red eyes of rats. There seemed to be no end to them as they spilled through the doorway and fanned out to encircle us, their furry brown bodies leaping all over each other in their haste to gain entrance to the little room. They came by the hundreds until the scratching of their claws on the stone floor became a continuous whisper and the sounds that issued from their tiny throats was like the chirping of birds in an aviary. Holmes and I began firing at the same time, advancing as we did so and scattering the loathsome rodents so that a narrow path was opened up in the heaving throng through which we hurried, firing as we went. I did not look back, for I knew even as we advanced that the path was closing behind us like water rushing back in to fill the gap left by the passage of a swift cutter. When we reached the top of the stairs we broke into a run, and did not slow down until we were outside of the building.

We were a block away from the estate and on our way to catch the train home before either of us trusted himself to speak. It was Holmes who broke the silence.

"It would appear that Dracula still commands armies," said he, excitedly. "I think we may consider our siege thoroughly repulsed."

I shuddered. "Ghastly beasts!"

"Ghastly indeed, and for a purpose. That little demonstration was designed to frighten us off, with great success. Even so we have won a victory."

"In what way? We did nothing."

"On the contrary, we have determined that the Count has other hiding places. Otherwise we would have found all fifty boxes of earth in the chapel."

"And how does that help us?"

He did not appear to have heard the question, intent as he was upon following the progress of a high, black brougham rattling down the street in the direction of Carfax. As it passed near a street lamp I saw that it contained five men, among whom was a strong, bespectacled profile which I recognised immediately.

"Van Helsing!" I exclaimed, in a whisper.

The detective nodded. "He has an extra man with him. Jonathan Harker has evidently finished his business at Whitby. I daresay that the professor and his companions are in for a reception much like the one given to us." We ducked into the shadows until they had passed, then continued on our way.

"You see, Watson," said Holmes when we were back at 221B and sharing a bottle of whisky, "now is when the true detective work begins. We know that Dracula has other lairs and it is up to us to find them. Once we have accomplished this, it should be a simple matter to dispose of his precious Transylvanian soil, thus narrowing his opportunities of exploiting this teeming isle."

"And if we should find the fiend himself?"

His expression was sober. "Then we must destroy him before he can spread his vampire pestilence throughout the Empire. We have no other choice."

The silence that settled in upon the completion of this statement was interrupted by a knock at the door.

"That's odd," I remarked, rising from the table. "I heard no footsteps upon the stairs." I set down my glass and went over to open the door. When I did so, I was struck speech less by the singular appearance of this late-night visitor.

He was garbed entirely in black, his only concession to colour being the silver crook of the massive black cane he carried in one talon-like hand. His face was elongated and high-browed, tilted upward in the manner of a member of a long and noble line, and pale almost to the point of translucence. His eyes glowed like smouldering embers beneath a pair of brows so wild and bushy that they almost met above the arch of his nose. So black was the unruly shock of hair that topped his high-domed head that it would have been lost in the midnight shadows behind his back were it not for the single streak of steely grey shooting up like a streak of lightning from the centre of the ragged widow's peak. All these things, combined with a height rather over six feet, would have made him an arresting figure in any company. But it was his teeth, the dagger-sharp canine teeth peeping out from beneath his drooping moustache, that held my attention. They were the fangs of a predator. I became convinced that to open the door to this creature was to invite all the terrors of the primordial night to invade the sanctity of our Baker Street digs. If ever there were a man who breathed death, it was the visitor who stood upon our threshold. All my instincts screamed for me to slam the door upon this vile apparition, to cast it back into the blackness whence it came and blot it from my memory. Instead, I found myself stepping aside to allow it to enter.

The stranger's eyes looked past me as if I were the merest lackey, to fall full upon those of my friend, who had risen to meet their cold stare.

"Mr. Sherlock Holmes?" His voice was as deep and devoid of emotion as the bass note of an organ in a cathedral. The detective nodded.

"I am Count Dracula."

Chapter Eight

The Hunt Begins

For perhaps a full minute after our visitor had introduced himself, no one moved. I am convinced that this was not due to any surprise upon the part of my friend, for from the moment the tall stranger appeared on the threshold his identity was never in doubt. Rather, I got the impression that the antagonists were measuring each other in anticipation of the struggle that would inevitably ensue. That I was considered little more than an interested spectator, and thus beneath the notice of the lordly presence in the doorway, was obvious from the start. At the end of the minute, the imperious expression upon the Count's face softened somewhat and he favoured Sherlock Holmes with a courtly bow. In so doing he nearly swept the floor with the high silk hat he held in his right hand.

"I am honoured to make your acquaintance, Sir," said he, in that organ-pipe bass which was only slightly tainted with the accent of the eastern hordes. "Even in the country of my birth we have been fortunate enough to read of your marvellous exploits against the English criminal. The impressive abilities you have demonstrated within your chosen field of endeavour are without equal anywhere upon the Continent."

It may have been that I was overwrought by his unexpected presence in our chambers, but I felt certain that he had placed a certain stress upon the words "your chosen field of endeavour." If Holmes had noticed this as well, he made no mention of it, but inclined his head in a bow of appreciation.

"You flatter me, Count. Your reputation precedes you as well."

There was no hostility in his tone, but it was there, in his words. The Count ignored it. He smiled in reply, exposing still further the razor-sharp canines which made my blood run cold just to look at them.

"The night is cold and I am not as young as once I was," he said. "May I come in?"

"Please do. Perhaps you would care to join my colleague and myself in some whisky. Watson, a glass."

"Thank you. I do not drink alcoholic beverages." Dracula closed the door behind him noiselessly and advanced farther into the room. I noticed that he towered over my friend by nearly four inches. "If it please you, I will stand," said he when Holmes indicated one of the armchairs. "The hours of the night are few, and I have many appointments to keep before morning. I will state my business and then you will be rid of me."

"Would that that were true, Count Dracula." Holmes returned his smile.

Dracula's expression grew cold. "You are an outspoken young man, Mr. Holmes, In my country that is a dangerous trait. I advise you to guard your tongue in my presence."

"My dear Count, we are both too old to waste time upon these pleasantries. How may I be of service to you?"

"Earlier this evening, you paid a visit to my home. I would like to know why."

"I think we both know the answer to that question," said my friend.

The visitor nodded ponderously. "So we do. I merely wished to hear your explanation, but you have side-stepped the issue most expertly.

"Before leaving Transylvania I made it a point to read as much as I could about the country to which I was moving. Among the many books and periodicals I gathered for this purpose was a number of yellow-backed journals containing Dr. Watson's accounts of the criminal cases you have solved thus far in your career. When I learned that it was you who had invaded my Purfleet residence, I realised that my activities in England had attracted your professional interest, an interest which I can hardly afford at this stage in my operations. I am here to ask you to abandon your investigations before they do real harm."

Holmes lit a cigarette and sent a cloud of smoke uncurling in the Count's direction. "If that is your purpose, then I am afraid that you have come all this way for nothing."

"I am a wealthy man, Mr. Holmes. I promise that you will not regret having granted me this one favour." The smoke failed to affect Dracula's composure. I wondered idly if he breathed at all.

Holmes said nothing.

A light came into the nobleman's eyes that disturbed me. I had seen that same glint in the eyes of the dread Hound of Hell just before it had leapt for the throat of Sir Henry Baskerville near Grimpen Mire in a year too close for comfort.

"I urge you to think it over." His voice was quietly threatening. "You think that you have faced all the terrors that the world has to offer, Sherlock Holmes, but you have barely scratched the surface. Jonathan Harker was driven mad by but a few of the myriad forces that are mine to command. He was fortunate. Even as we stand here, those forces are gathering, responding to my unspoken instructions with but one purpose in mind: to destroy all obstacles which stand in my path. From icy graves they arise, from gallows and tombs, for all that die are my agents. They are the army of the dead. How may one mortal expect to triumph over such an enemy?"

"Bogey tales ceased to frighten me many years ago," said the detective. "I am no more affected by them than I was by your rats."

"The rats were a warning. I assure you that when I decide to act in earnest, you will not escape."

"I think I have heard enough. You may show our visitor the door, Watson."

"That will not be necessary." Gathering his cloak about him, Count Dracula turned and swung open the door. Halfway through the doorway he stopped and fixed Holmes with a bestial glance. "There are far worse things than death, Mr. Holmes. Persist, and I promise that you will find out what I mean." He went out and closed the door behind him.

I was seized with a sudden impulse to make certain that he had left. The door was barely shut before I hurried over and tore it open, releasing a flood of light into the darkened hallway. There was no one there.

"Close the door, Watson; there's a draught."

When I had done as directed, Holmes strode over to the hearth, seized a poker, and fell to stirring the flames in the fireplace. "Do you notice it, Watson?" said he. "A physical sensation of cold, as if all the windows were suddenly flung open and the fire was doused with water? I felt the same thing the moment we entered Carfax, though we were stepping in from the chill of the night. It is the miasma that surrounds Count Dracula. There; it grows warmer now that he has left."

"I did notice a chill, now that you mention it."

"A most informative confrontation. What do you suppose he thought to accomplish by coming here?" He rose from his crouched position before the fireplace and returned the poker to its rack.

"I should think that is obvious," I replied. "He hoped to persuade you to stop interfering with his plans. When bribery failed, he resorted to threats."

He shook his head, smiling. "I doubt that anyone who has read your descriptions of my sterling character would seek to buy me off a case with mere money. Furthermore, threats of a nature as general as those he delivered are so seldom heeded that I can hardly believe he expected them to be effective. No, Watson, Dracula had no intention of inducing me to leave him alone. That was merely his excuse to come here and observe his enemy in his natural habitat. Which is the same reason you and I invaded his domain at Purfleet earlier this evening."

"And what do you suppose he has gained?"

"If nothing else, the ability to recognise me when next I cross his path. You noticed, of course, that he never took his eyes off me during the entire visit."

"I could not help but notice." I shuddered. "And what eyes! More those of a beast than of a man."

"I quite agree. A most savage and cunning beast is Count Dracula, whose fangs and claws are all the more dangerous because of the mighty brain which directs them. It is with hesitancy that I contemplate his destruction."

I frowned disapprovingly. "I have never known you to be hesitant in the face of danger, Holmes."

"Not for myself, Watson. It is for your wonderful wife that I fear. I do not wish to make her a widow before her time."

"I did not demur before a dangerous undertaking when I was a bachelor, Holmes. I see no reason to do so now that I am a married man. I assure you that, were she here right now, my wife would agree that it is my duty to assist you in any way that I can."

Again he smiled. "I expected no less. Very well, since you insist upon following me along this foolhardy path, I suggest that you call down to Mrs. Hudson and ask her to prepare us a large pot of black coffee which will keep us awake while we draw up a plan of action."

The night wore on and the level of coffee in the pot grew low as we attacked the problem from every angle. It seemed evident to me that the best way to deal with the vampire was to go to Carfax on the morrow and destroy him while he slept in his native earth, but Holmes disagreed. "He would possess much less intelligence than I have given him credit for if he returned to the estate now," said he. "Tomorrow I shall pay another visit to Whitby, where for a few crowns I should be able to find out from the men who delivered them where the remainder of the fifty boxes were sent. Where they are, Dracula cannot be far away."

"I will ask Mrs. Hudson to knock us up early," said I, rising from the table. Holmes waved me back into my seat.

"My dear fellow, your company is always appreciated, but in this instance hardly necessary. Why waste money upon two tickets when one will suffice? I will be back by nightfall, and then we will discuss our next step. In the meantime, I think we could both do with a good night's sleep."

In spite of the cavalier fashion in which my friend had dismissed the fiend's visit, it was obvious that the episode had unnerved him; twice I awoke during the night to hear the melancholy strains of one of Holmes's excellent compositions coming from his violin in the sitting room, a sure sign that he was too pre-occupied with the problem at hand to sleep. At such times it was best to leave him alone, for I knew from long association that no amount of scolding would persuade him to rest properly until it was solved. It was probable that he would sleep during the train ride to Whitby anyway. My conscience thus salved, I rolled over and returned to my own uneasy dreams. I hardly need add that they were filled with Bloofer Ladies and sinister noblemen.

Holmes was gone when I got up the next morning, but he had left a note for me upon the sideboard.

> Watson,
>
> Mrs. Hudson has instructions to open all my correspondence and will get in touch with me should anything of import arise. Suggest that you spend the day with Mrs. Watson. Strongly suggest that you bring flowers.
>
> S.H.

I took his advice, and, after presenting my wife with a bouquet of chrysanthemums from her favourite florist, took her to lunch and then to a program at Shoreditch Music Hall. I am afraid that I left most of the conversation up to her during the stroll back, for I was reluctant to frighten her with the details of our present adventure. The next few hours were spent quietly at home. When it came time for me to leave, the tone of my wife's admonition to "be careful" left me wondering if in her intuitive fashion she had somehow divined the grim nature of the mission upon which Holmes and I were engaged, despite my efforts to keep it a secret. She knew me better than any person alive.

The sitting room was dark when I reached Baker Street, as was indeed the rest of the building. Deciding that Mrs. Hudson had retired, I unlocked the front door and went up to wait for Holmes. I had barely finished lighting the lamps when the door opened and in slouched a common loafer. He was dressed in rags and smoking the stub of a cigarette so short that it was difficult to imagine how he could leave it dangling from between his lips without igniting the stubble upon his chin. So convincing was his threadbare appearance that I had to take a hard look at him to be sure that it was Sherlock Holmes. In another minute there was no longer any question of it, for he had doffed the worn felt hat which had concealed his intelligent brow and assumed that smug expression I had so often noted upon my friend's countenance when he was certain of victory. The effect was somewhat lessened by a purple bruise which had swollen his left eye almost shut.

"My dear Holmes!" I exclaimed concernedly. "What has happened? You look as if you have been involved in the lowest form of street brawl."

"Exactly! Your powers of observation increase daily." He smiled more broadly, wincing when the alteration in his expression affected his injured eye.

"It is fortunate that this time I thought to take along my bag," said I, opening it. "Sit down. You can tell me all about it while I treat that bruise."

"Later, Watson. First allow me to shave and change into the attire of a respectable gentleman. Then you may apply all the miracles of modern medical science to this badge of success and I will recount for your benefit the details of a most interesting day."

He went to his bedroom, to return a quarter of an hour later shaved and wearing the old purple dressing-gown he preferred to any other form of attire. By that time I had prepared a mild solution of soapy water with, which I cleansed the contusion while he sat in his armchair and began his narrative.

"I really have little reason to smile," said he, closing his eyes lest the soap sting them, "for I am guilty of a capital error that has very nearly cost both of us our lives. Until now I have been proceeding upon the assumption that Dracula is a lone figure and that we outnumber him two to one. Yet by his own testimony, we know that the Count is a wealthy man; is it so difficult, then, to imagine that he has purchased the loyalty of a sizeable number of agents throughout England? It is an elementary assumption, and yet I confess that it escaped me until it was literally drummed into my skull this afternoon near Whitby harbour.

"I had just left the office of the manager of our nation's leading transport firm when a pair of brutes in ragged pea jackets overtook me in an alley and one of them delivered a right to my eye, the evidence of which is still painfully apparent. Had it not been for my stick and a thorough knowledge of the Japanese style of wrestling, I might even now be lying in that same alley in a pool of my own blood. I am happy to say that after experiencing a couple of tumbles both gentlemen were intelligent enough to take to their heels. Nevertheless, the incident left its impression upon me, in more ways than one.

"What a fool I have been, Watson! I fear that my reputation will suffer among your readers when you publish this account, and yet it is no more than I deserve for having under-estimated our enemy so severely. I was, of course, followed after leaving here, and when it was determined where I was headed, Dracula's agents in Whitby were notified to intercept me there and administer a somewhat more stringent warning to remind me of the one I received last night."

"You seem to be in rather good spirits in spite of it," I observed, gently patting dry the inflamed area around his left eye.

"And why not? I have learned all of Dracula's hiding places in London."

"From whom?"

"From the gentleman in the transport office, just before I was assaulted. Fortunately he keeps a record of each of his firm's deliveries on file down to the last collar button. On August tenth his employees placed all fifty boxes of earth upon a train for London, escorted them into the city, and placed them in four separate locations according to the instructions of their client. Among these locations is Carfax Estate."

"We will, I assume, visit each of the places mentioned?" I applied tincture of iodine to a triangular abrasion-evidence of a bony knuckle–at the top of his cheekbone and wiped off the excess with a wad of cotton. He did not flinch, although the sting must have been terrific.

"On the contrary, we will do nothing."

"*Nothing*?" I nearly dropped the bottle of iodine.

"We would only be covering territory which has already been covered. I learned during my inquiries that another gentleman had been there before me; I can only assume that this was Jonathan Harker. No doubt he has already imparted the information to Van Helsing and company, and they are even now returning from a most productive day spent in destroying Dracula's places of rest. Why gild the lily?"

"Then Dracula is finished."

"I doubt that, Watson," he replied morosely. "I doubt that very much."

I returned my equipment to the black bag and angrily snapped it shut.

"I fail to understand you, Holmes. You begin by counselling inaction, and then you tell me that England is still at the mercy of this hideous creature. I have never known you to be so apathetic in the face of such a crisis."

He laughed.

"I see no humour in the situation," I exploded.

"My dear fellow, I have done you a great injustice." He stood up and placed a hand upon my shoulder. "The Count is growing nervous. Why else would he have set those ruffians upon me, knowing full well that they were no match for one of my experience? It was, as I said earlier, a mere warning. More specifically, it was an act of desperation, and you and I both know that desperate men make mistakes. This is what I meant when I suggested that we do nothing; I should have made clear the fact that we will be waiting."

"Waiting? For what?"

"For Count Dracula to make his first mistake. I assure you, Watson, that it will be his last as well."

We stood in silence for a long time, Holmes with his hand on my shoulder, myself with my fists doubled up in my pockets. I think that both of us were thinking the same thing as we gazed out into the blackness beyond the window. We were wondering who would die before the night was over.

Chapter Nine

DRACULA MAKES A MISTAKE

I have never known my friend Sherlock Holmes to be more reclusive and difficult to talk to than he was during the opening days of October 1890. As hour followed upon hour with no news that would give us a clue to the progress of Count Dracula's activities, the detective withdrew into a shell of secrecy and quietude that even I could not hope to crack, and I daresay that more than one prospective client left his quarters during this period in a huff over the cool reception they had met inside. It was not until four o'clock on the afternoon of the third, when a blond-bearded messenger appeared at our door with a note addressed to him, that Holmes so far unbent himself as to speak to me in words of more than a single syllable.

"It's from Lestrade," he declared, scanning the hastily scrawled missive. "He wishes to see us. Get on your coat, Watson. This could be the news for which we have been waiting." He dismissed the messenger and tore off his dressing-gown on the way to the coat rack. From it he drew his jacket, the familiar Inverness, and cap.

"Where are we headed?" I slipped my ulster and billycock from the rack and donned them.

"To the Whitechapel mortuary, where the inspector awaits us."

We seemed destined always to meet the egotistical detective from Scotland Yard among the most dismal surroundings. In the affair which I have detailed under the title of *A Study in Scarlet*, the first in which I accompanied my remarkable friend, we had spoken with Lestrade in the dilapidated room where the murdered man lay at Number 3, Lauriston Gardens; since then we had encountered him amidst varying degrees of squalor and in circumstances of the darkest nature, so that it did not seem in the least strange when we found him standing inside the ugly white-washed entrance-way of the East End mortuary. His face, normally long, reminded me in this instance of an old workhorse whose only future lay in the glue factory. It did not brighten as we approached.

"I am glad that you could make it, Holmes," said he, in a tone at once listless and grudging, as if he lamented having had to call us in at all. "This is a most serious business we are involved in today. A most serious business indeed."

"What's up, then?" asked my friend in his brisk manner.

"Our very worst nightmares have come true. The Ripper is up to his old tricks."

"A mistake, certainly!" I exclaimed in my shock.

Lestrade shook his head gravely. "I wish it was, Dr. Watson, but the evidence is all too conclusive."

"Where is the victim?" Holmes asked.

"In the back." The little man turned and led us into the mortuary proper.

I make no pretense that I did not shrink inwardly when we entered the presence of the many sheet-wrapped corpses lying upon tables in the huge main room. Rather than inuring me, the years which I had spent as a physician on top of my experiences as a surgeon in Afghanistan had made me extremely sensitive to the sight of death and dying, and the experience of suddenly finding myself in the presence of so much mortality was far from pleasant. Nor was the design of the room meant to make the scene any more palatable, for the walls, like those of the entrance-way, were white-washed and bare, and smelled strongly of carbolic acid. Even the sunlight flooding in through the high windows near the ceiling seemed unnaturally harsh, glaring as it did from the blank white walls. A sober-faced attendant stood at the head of an occupied table at the far end of the room. It was to this table that Lestrade was heading.

When he had stopped, the inspector nodded to the attendant and the sheet was pulled from the corpse. I nearly vomited when I saw what some fiend had done to the poor girl who lay naked upon the table.

"Replace the sheet." Holmes's voice was strained.

Lestrade nodded a second time, and once again the body was covered.

"Who was she?" There was suppressed anger in my friend's tone now. He was as outraged as I at the thought of the creature capable of such a hideous crime being allowed to roam the streets in freedom.

"A prostitute by the name of Rachel North," replied the inspector. "She was known among the patrons of the local pubs as Randy Rachel, and was much beloved of the street urchins for the stories she used to make up to keep the tykes entertained. A policeman found her slumped inside a doorway in the next street from here at three o'clock this morning; she'd been dead at least an hour by then."

"What makes you think that this is the work of Jack the Ripper?"

Lestrade snorted. "Well, now, what do you suppose makes me

think that? Who but old Leather Apron himself would slash an inoffensive prostitute's throat and leave her to drown in her own blood?"

"Her throat was more than slashed, Inspector. It was torn clean out, and by a much less tidy instrument than a knife. And how do you explain the absence of any other wounds upon her body? Where is that skilful dissection upon which the Ripper prided himself?"

"I imagine he was interrupted before he could finish," countered the other, but with less confidence than he had evinced earlier.

Holmes shook his head. "It won't stand up. Why was not the body found until three o'clock this morning, if the culprit were surprised in the act an hour before? As for your theory that she drowned in her own blood, how can you reconcile that with the fact that there is very little blood to be found either in the wound or upon the corpse? Or has the Ripper found a new souvenir to take home with him?"

Lestrade was piqued. "I suppose you have a theory that will cover all the facts," he challenged.

"I have a theory, but I doubt very strongly that you will believe it. Let us be off, Watson. It is growing dark and our time is short." He turned to leave.

"You don't mean to say that you are giving up on the case?" sputtered Lestrade. He seemed torn between disbelief and satisfaction.

"I mean to say that we are leaving. My advice to you, Inspector, is to abandon any preconceptions you may have formed regarding the Ripper's involvement in this case. We stalk a far more dangerous and cunning foe."

The Scotland Yard detective drew himself up to his full height–which was not much–and presented Holmes with a most supercilious expression. "And my advice to, you, Mr. Sherlock Holmes, is to keep your advice to yourself. The Yard is quite capable of apprehending its criminals without your help. I invited you in today merely because I knew that this is the sort of thing that interests you, but I can see that it is quite over your head. Good day to you both."

Holmes was chuckling when we stepped from that place of death into the scarcely more cheerful atmosphere of the East End street. "Lestrade never ceases to astound me," he confided. "Each time I see him he has grown more stubborn and unimaginative than he was the time before. There seems to be no limit to his ignorance."

"Do you think it was Dracula who mutilated that poor woman?" The sight of Rachel North's horribly torn throat still floated before my vision.

"Who else? It was unlike him, however, to have made such an untidy job of it. I can only think that he is desperate and in a hurry, else he would have taken pains to see that the body was never found. I think, Watson, that Dracula is preparing to leave."

"Leave? For where?"

He shrugged. "I cannot say. Transylvania, perhaps. But I doubt it."

"It would seem a wise choice under the circumstances."

"And yet it is not like the Count to give up so easily. He may alter his plans, but it is doubtful that he would reverse them simply because they are known to his enemies. No, Watson; I fear that whatever form Dracula's next step takes, it will not be surrender."

"As long as we are on the subject of the next step," said I, "what form will our own take?"

Holmes looked thoughtful. "Tell me, Doctor," he said at last. "Why do you suppose our quarry chose Whitechapel as a place to strike, when he had all London from which to choose?"

I considered the question. "Perhaps because here the prey is easiest," I remarked after a moment.

"A distinct possibility. Can you think of any others? No? Consider this: Does the lion ever hunt for food beyond the immediate vicinity of his home?"

Slowly my friend's reasoning dawned upon me. "Never!" I exclaimed. "Do you think–?"

"As often as possible. Considering Dracula's preference for abandoned buildings, we should have little difficulty in locating a suitable place within a half-mile radius. We had best get started, for darkness is nearly upon us. I need hardly caution you about the capabilities of a cornered beast."

The number of empty buildings in London's squalid East End was phenomenal. We spent the next two hours investigating the empty shells of taverns and public houses which had been unable either to compete with their hundreds of rivals or to conceal their own nefarious activities from the police, with little result other than to soil our clothes with cob-webs and dust. There was no sign of our quarry in any of them. We were emerging from one of these filthy caves when Holmes stopped suddenly and announced that we had been going about our search all wrong.

"This is a fine time to realise it," I said testily, brushing thick brown dust from the crown of my hat.

"I do not deny that I should have reached the conclusion sooner," he apologised. "Cluttered as these establishments are, none of them has been empty for more than a year, and any are liable to be entered by a prospective buyer at any time. Yet we know from experience that Dracula prefers to set up housekeeping in long-abandoned quarters where his chances of being discovered are not so high. Does that suggest anything to you?"

"I should think that a condemned building would be ideal for his purposes," I ventured.

"Precisely! We will make a detective of you yet. There is a building nearby which once sheltered a slaughter-house, but which has been empty for no short time. It was recently condemned. What better hiding place could there be for such a murderer? Come, Watson; there is no time to waste." He hailed a passing hansom and was inside it before the driver had a chance to stop.

The butchery was an imposing one-storey edifice of brick, which occupied an entire block at Whitechapel's lower end, its barren yard surrounded by a dilapidated wooden fence upon which local wags had inscribed words and slogans of varying degrees of vulgarity in charcoal and chalk. The huge square windows which encircled the walls of the building were boarded up, lending the structure a blank appearance that was most malevolent under the circumstances and contributing to the indistinct nature of the hulking black shadow it formed against the scarcely lighter hue of the sky. The gate was open when we got there.

"It should be locked tight," observed my companion in a low whisper. "He is here, Watson."

The chilling effect which these words instilled in me was heightened by the realisation that strange *sounds* were issuing from within the enclosure. I say "strange" not because the noises–thumps and squeaks and miscellaneous rattles–were in themselves out of the ordinary, but rather because of the stillness everywhere else that made them so much more evident than they would have seemed amidst other surroundings. That some activity was being performed among the shadows was obvious; that it boded ill because it was connected with the undead thing we stalked was no less apparent. I was prepared for anything when we passed through the yawning maw of the opened gate and onto the much-bloodied grounds.

At first the amber glow of the single lantern that hung from a nail in the front door of the building was the only thing I saw. As I grew accustomed to the unexpected illumination, however, I began to make out the other objects and figures standing within the beaten yard: the waggon with its team of two coal-black horses, pointed towards the gate; the pair of burly workmen struggling to lift a heavy object into the bed of the waggon–the rectangular crate, so like its twenty-nine fellows we had seen in Carfax; and, directing the operation, his back turned towards us, the black-cloaked figure of the Count himself. At our appearance the workmen paused in their labour to stare at us. This caught Dracula's attention. Slowly he turned.

The expression of fury which seized his features upon recognising us was a thing to behold. His eyes were aflame beneath the iron arch of his brow, seeming in their incandescence to further blacken the deep shadows that hollowed his cheeks and carved sharp scores from his nostrils to the corners of his mouth. The long canines I had noted upon our first meeting were bared in a threatening snarl, the curled upper lip violent red against the black of his moustache. His breathing was sibilant and rapid. He was hatless, and a lock of his raven hair had fallen over one side of his forehead, thus contributing to the over-all bestiality of his appearance. In that instant I was reminded of Holmes's warning of two hours before: that Count Dracula cornered was a thing to be feared.

"Fools!" The epithet was like an explosion, echoing from the wall of the slaughter-house like the treble of the organ in the rafters of the cathedral. "What brainless idiots you are, to have come all this way to die."

Our adversary's rage was not lost upon Holmes, whose own features had grown taut in the face of the diatribe. Nevertheless, he stood his ground. In his right hand glittered the silver crucifix with which he had saved me from the fangs of the Bloofer Lady in the days when the supernatural was nothing more than a word. "Hollow words, Count." His voice was calm as ice. "Instruct your servants to unload the box."

Dracula's anger was a tangible thing. In its presence the muscular workmen had fallen back until now they were flattened against the brick wall of the building. Neither of them moved.

It was then that the Count acted.

In a single bound he traversed the five yards that separated us, and with a backward sweep of his powerful right arm knocked Holmes off his feet, sending the crucifix flying. When I rushed forward to stop the fiend, the Count placed his left hand against my chest and hurled me backwards with no more effort than it takes to push away a child's India-rubber balloon. I lost my balance and fell into the dirt. By this time Dracula had leapt up onto the waggon and, seizing the reins in one hand and the whip in the other, sent the latter uncurling over the backs of the frightened horses. They whinnied and bolted forward. I barely had time to realise that they were going to run over me, and to thrust my arms up over my face, before they were there. Hooves pounded past on both sides, the waggon clattered overhead, and then I was alone amidst the settling dust. I did not uncover my face until I heard Holmes's voice calling my name over and over excitedly.

"Watson!" he cried, seizing my shoulders and shaking me. "Watson, are you all right?" There was a note of fear in his tone.

I brought down my arms and propped myself up on one elbow, peering at him through the dust and the darkness. "He's escaped, Holmes," I said defeatedly.

He laughed in his relief. "I would rather have him escape a hundred times than have you harmed once, dear friend. But cease your worrying. We will find him soon enough."

"Indeed?" I climbed to my feet with the aid of Holmes's outstretched hand and dusted myself off. A quick glance around satisfied me that the two workmen had fled. "And how do you propose to do that?"

"Do you recall the affair of Jonathan Small and his diminutive partner, and how we tracked them through London's busy streets?" There was an impish glint in his eye.

"Toby?"

He nodded. "A dog with a nose for criminals. He should have little trouble following the path of so clumsy a mode of transportation as a waggon."

"I seem to recall that Small's accomplice had stepped in some creosote which was of no little aid in allowing the dog to sniff the two of them out," I reminded him. "How do you expect Toby to be able to differentiate between the tracks left by this waggon and those of the thousands of other vehicles which have passed along the streets within the past few hours?"

"Come now, Watson. Have you forgotten where we are?"

"A slaughter-house. But what–"

"And you are telling me that any self-respecting dog would find it difficult to track down a waggon whose wheels have rolled over ground rich in blood and old entrails?" He smiled slyly.

"Holmes," I cried, "you are truly a genius!"

"My blushes, Watson!" said he, but his face was alight nonetheless. It was the last smile that was to cross either of our faces for a very long time.

Chapter Ten

A Horrible Revelation

"I've fifty dogs in these 'ere kennels that'll make short work of you unless you leave this premises, you filthy prowler!"

Those who have read my description of the events which were connected with "the sign of four" will recall that old Mr. Sherman, who owned the remarkable dog Toby, was not the most hospitable of men. Therefore I was not surprised when in answer to my knock at the door of his shabby Pinchin Lane residence I heard his cracked voice threatening me with all manner of bodily harm if I did not remove my presence.

"It's Dr. Watson, Mr. Sherman," I said.

"I don't care if it's Queen Victoria! Away wi' you! I've a mad terrier in 'ere, and I'll set 'im on your throat if I don't 'ear your footsteps goin' away." The aged face at the upper window looked satanic in the light of the single candle he held beneath his chin.

"I've come for a dog."

"Aye, and a dog is what you'll get! 'E'll bite you, 'e will, and you'll die a screamin', ravin' death because you didn't leave when old

Sherman told you to! I'll give you thirty seconds, and then it's open wi' the door and out wi' the terrier."

"Mr. Sherlock Holmes–"

I knew from my earlier experience that the name was all I needed to gain entry, but I'd forgotten how quickly it worked. Immediately the window banged shut and a moment later the door swung wide. Inside stood Mr. Sherman, lankier and leaner even than I remembered him, bent almost double now beneath the weight of his years and blinking myopically behind the thick blue-tinted lenses of his spectacles. His wrinkled face was split in two by what he presumably thought was an ingratiating smile.

"Forgive me, Doctor," said he, standing aside so that I could enter. "I didn't recognise the name till you mentioned Mr. Sherlock. Step in, sir."

I edged in cautiously. "Where is the mad terrier?"

He cackled. "Bless you, sir, that was a little invention of my own. I didn't know but that you might be one of those brats what come around of a night just to knock me up. The badger there is real, though, and 'e bites, so I advise you to steer 'im a wide berth. Is it Toby you've come for?"

"Yes. We have need of his talents."

"That would be Number Seven."

Turning, he led the way with his candle along a line of kennels that stretched the length of the ground floor to our left, most of which were occupied by dogs of every size and type who bounded to the front of their cages to yap at us. Other enclosures contained birds and reptiles and sundry wild creatures whose eyes shone pale green in the light of the moving candle, while above our heads every inch of rafter space was taken up by owls and other types of fowl. From Kennel Number 7 Sherman released the ugly, lop-eared creature without whose help we would never have apprehended the men responsible for the death of my wife's father in the days of my bachelorhood. Toby wagged his tail in happy recognition when I patted him on the head.

"I can see 'e remembers you, sir," observed the old naturalist. "No need for the lump of sugar this time."

"Good dog, Toby."

"More than good, Doctor; 'e's the best. Give my regards to Mr. Sherlock, and mind the badger on your way out."

A short cab ride brought us back to Whitechapel, where Holmes awaited us in front of the butchery. He was smoking his pipe amidst a spreading fog.

"There's a good dog," he said when Toby was before him, whining ecstatically and wagging his tail at the sight of his old friend. "A bit overfed, but we'll run off some of that excess baggage." Holmes straightened. "I have just completed my search of Dracula's last place of residence," he informed me.

"And what have you found?"

"Very little." He reached into his coat pocket and handed me a small disc of gleaming metal. "What do you make of that?"

I examined the object in the light of the lantern the Count had left hanging upon the door. It was a gold coin, roughly the size of a crown and stamped with an effigy I did not recognise. There was foreign writing on both sides. "A rouble?" I guessed.

"Roubles are silver. As near as I can surmise, it's a Hungarian coin, issued about the time of the Turko-Magyar wars in the late fifteenth century. I found it wedged into a crack in the floor near the entrance."

"What does it mean?" I handed it back.

"I hardly imagine that Dracula carries a good luck charm; therefore it is part of the working capital he brought with him from Transylvania. Since it was the only coin there, it naturally follows that he is carrying the rest upon his person. Which means that he is leaving England."

"Then we have won!" I rejoiced.

His face did not reflect my optimism. "Have we? Perhaps. In any case, I will feel much better once we have determined that he is on his way back to Transylvania and not towards some new conquest. How about it, fellow? Are you up to a chase?"

"I have never been more prepared for one."

"Sniff the ground, Toby!" he told the dog. "What do you think of that, boy? Smell it, Toby, smell it!"

In response to my friend's gestures, the shaggy detective placed his broad wet snout against the dark earth, and, snuffing loudly, began racing all about the yard, his tail quivering. Holmes produced a stout cord and fastened it to the dog's collar. Almost immediately Toby launched into a series of strident yelps and strained at the leash, pulling Holmes in the direction of the gate.

"Come along, Watson!" he called over his shoulder. "Time and Toby wait for no man."

We must have made quite a sight for the early-evening strollers in Whitechapel and beyond, one middle-aged man being pulled along by a whooping mongrel whilst another hurried along in their path, puffing and holding onto his hat with one hand. Certainly we turned our share of heads as we shouldered our way through the crowds on the street, especially once, when we came close to knocking down a street peddler, prompting curses upon his part and causing him, I am sure, to shake his fist angrily at our retreating backs. Still we hastened onward.

I grew uneasy as we emerged from the twisting dark alleys of the East End and entered more familiar surroundings. I think that this was because the thought of a creature like Dracula haunting the same streets that were travelled by fashionable society was so abhorrent to my sensibilities. That something so vile and depraved as a vampire should skulk about the decaying scenery of Whitechapel seemed almost fitting and proper; that it should leave those surroundings for those in which I myself practised was nothing short of sacrilege. I can scarcely express the extent of the outrage which gripped me when I thought of this denizen of darkness presuming to prey upon the most civilised society on earth. For the first and only time in my life, I felt the urge to kill.

As for Sherlock Holmes, any emotions which he may have entertained concerning the present venture were subjugated by his infatuation with the hunt. I have already described the change which came over his features when he was in hot pursuit; suffice it to say that in this case there was little difference between his profile and that of the eager dog straining and yelping at the other end of the leash I doubt that he was even conscious of the startled strollers with whom he was perpetually in danger of colliding during our headlong dash across London, so engrossed was he in his quest. His eyes were like tiny suns.

Onwards we ran, through gangs of people and across all lanes of traffic, following the spoor of death. Opportunities to rest were few and short-lived. Again, as during that mad cab ride of several days before, we ignored the police whistles shrieking all about us as of little importance in comparison with what was at stake, even as we ignored the hazards of rushing through a thickening fog that turned the gaslamps into swollen globes of ineffectual light and masked the obstacles in our path. Nor did it matter to Toby, for whom nothing existed beyond the encouraging odour of the East End slaughter-house. Our pace slackened not a whit.

How can I describe the cold sensation that began to gnaw at my vitals when the trail veered towards my own neighbourhood? It was like the feeling one gets when, returning home, he spies a column of smoke rising above his street and wonders if it is his own house that is burning. I told myself that my fears were groundless, that it was most likely nearby Paddington Station to which the fiend was heading, there to book passage elsewhere, but still I feared. Had not my wife experienced terrors enough in her young life, without having to face this blackest of nightmares as well?

We had gone scarcely another hundred yards when my worst apprehensions were realised. With a mighty lunge, the dog tore the leash from my friend's grip and bounded up the stairs of my building to where the front door stood halfway open. He disappeared inside, his triumphant barks echoing hollowly inside the entrance.

"Watson–" Holmes began, but stopped when he saw my face in the light of the gaslamp above my door.

So suddenly did Toby stop barking that I thought he had come to some harm. By this time I was halfway up the front stairs, taking them two at a time, forgetting my exhaustion and unmindful of whatever danger lay beyond the door. Holmes was right behind me. I nearly tripped over the dog, crouched as he was upon the linoleum with his head down and his tail tucked between his legs. He was whimpering piteously. At first I could see no reason for this curious behaviour on his part, but slowly I became aware of the strange and terrible aura that filled the still-lighted entranceway. I had felt it only twice before; the first time when Count Dracula paid us a visit in Holmes's rooms, and again when we had surprised him at the slaughter-house in Whitechapel. It was the unearthly chill that he took with him from the grave.

"He's been here, Holmes," I heard myself saying hollowly.

"Search the premises," he snapped. "Your wife may still be here."

We spent the next few minutes combing every room in the vain hope that Mary may have succeeded in hiding from the vampire's omniscient eye. My despair deepened with each failure. I had finished with the ground floor and was on my way up to the first when I heard Holmes's urgent voice calling me from the master bedroom. I fairly flew the rest of the way.

I found him standing in the middle of the room with his hand upon the shoulder of a slack-faced matron with frazzled grey hair and steel-rimmed spectacles which had a disconcerting habit of sliding down her nose, an aberration which she corrected by perpetually adjusting them with a nervous forefinger. Her plain brown dress was smeared with dust. She was shaking as if stricken with palsy.

"I came upon her cowering in the closet with her back to the door," Holmes reported. "She claims to be your neighbour."

"It is Mrs. Barton from next door." I lost control and seized her by the shoulders. "Where is my wife, Mrs. Barton?" I demanded. "What has happened to her?"

Holmes placed a restraining hand upon my arm. "Easy, Watson. She's had a bad enough time of it without your frightening her further. Have you brandy in the house?"

I nodded. "Downstairs, in the sitting room." The calmness of my friend's demeanour had taken the edge off my panic.

"Be a good fellow and set us up some glasses," he said. "We will follow you down."

Mrs. Barton proved to be suffering from a mild form of shock, but a few sips of the excellent brandy I had received as a gift of appreciation from one of my more affluent patients brought her around. She was no stranger to difficulty; the death of her husband, an infantryman of my acquaintance who fell during the battle of Maiwand, had left her nearly destitute, and it had only been through my efforts that she had been able to secure lodgings near ours at much lower rates.

Although her hand continued to shake, she seemed to understand the gentle questions Holmes put to her, and before long she launched into the following narrative, from which I have as usual taken the liberty of removing a number of vagaries and repetitions which might prove confusing to the reader. I need no notes to set it down much as I heard it, for every word has been burned indelibly into my memory, where it will remain until the day I die.

"Mrs. Watson had dismissed her maid for the evenin' and was feelin' poorly," she said, in a voice barely above a whisper. "I brought her some tea in the sittin' room. I'd not been visitin' ten minutes when the door busts open and in *He* comes." She shuddered. "Tall He was, and black, with eyes blazin' red as coals in a hearth–"

"One moment," Holmes broke in gently. "When you say that he was black, don't you mean that he was merely *dressed* in that colour?"

"Aye, sir, and that may be true, but it seemed to me then that He was black as Death himself, with nostrils flarin', and–saints preserve me–white fangs gleamin' in His blood-red mouth. He just comes in and stands there starin'. Mrs. Watson was in her robe and night-dress; she gathers them round and gets up from the table, demandin' to know who He is and what He's doin' here and how He got in. He smiles then, and that's when I sees His fangs.

"'You are Mary Watson,' He says. His voice give me the creeps, deep and slow like it was.

"'I am, says she. 'But who are you?'

"'Your husband is Dr. John Watson,' He says.

"Now she gets scared. 'Is it about John? Has something happened to him? Where is he?' She starts to run across the room, but she don't get five steps before she stops dead in front of Him. 'Who are you?' she says again.

"'I am your escort for the evenin',' says He.

"'I ordered no such escort. I don't know who you are, but I don't believe you're a friend of my husband. Where is he and what have you done to him?' When He don't say nothin', she turns to me and says, 'Mrs. Barton, summon the police.' That's when He starts laughin'.

"I know you will think me an awful coward, Doctor, but I was afraid to move from my place against the wall. His laugh was all cold and hollow, like it was echoin' inside a tomb. My hair like to've stood up on end at the sound of it. Suddenly He stopped, and His expression become grave.

"'My time is short and I have a long journey ahead of me,' He says. 'Come.' He grabs hold of her wrist and tries to pull her to Him, but she squirms, screamin' for me to call for the police. Even if I could move, though, it wouldn't've done no good, because in the next second the monster swung her up into His arms and carried her kickin' and screamin' to the door. On the threshold He stops and looks back at me. He had the Devil's own eyes, and they burned like all the fires of Hell was behind them. I thought it was all over for me.

"Mrs. Watson had fainted. He held her limp body like you or me might hold a wee one's rag doll. When He spoke to me, His voice was quiet. 'Inform the doctor that no harm will befall his mate if he and his friend do not follow,' says He. 'I hardly need to remind him what fate lies in store for her if they do.' Then He ups and vanishes into the fog at the top of the steps.

"I was scared He'd come back for me, so I run upstairs and hid myself in the closet. When I heard the door openin' I was sure He had me, but now I can see that the good Lord has spared me to light a candle for Mrs. Watson in church tonight, and that is just what I plan to do as soon as you gentlemen are through with me."

"Good lord, Holmes," I said, almost in a state of shock myself. "He has her. The fiend has my wife."

He placed a sympathetic hand upon my shoulder. "One more question, Mrs. Barton," he said. "Did he say anything about where he was going?"

She shook her head. "No, sir. But after He left, I thought I heard the wheels of a waggon or a four-wheeler rattlin' in the direction of King's Cross."

"I see. Thank you, Mrs. Barton. You have been most helpful." When she had taken her leave, swaying upon unsteady legs, Holmes picked up the decanter of brandy and poured out a stiff draught for each of us. "It is my belief that the Count is a man of his word," said he. "I have little doubt but that he will release Mrs. Watson unharmed if we do not follow."

"And then what?" I countered. "Whose wife will be his next victim? We cannot afford to let this vile thing remain upon the face of the earth, Holmes. We must crush him beneath our heels like the venomous insect he is. No matter what the cost."

"Even at the risk of your wife's soul?"

It was a few seconds before I found the nerve to answer. "Even so," I said.

Surprisingly, he smiled at this and smacked my shoulder with the palm of his hand. "Good old Watson! How can I help but take you for granted, when your character is so consistently strong?" He finished his brandy and rose from the table. "We will return Toby to his owner along with the price of a raw steak for a job well done, and then it's off to King's Cross Station. This tale will have a happy ending yet."

When we passed Mrs. Barton's rooms there was no light showing under her door. "Lighting a candle for Mrs. Watson, no doubt," observed my companion. "A devout woman."

"I hope she lights one for us as well," I said.

Chapter Eleven

Trail of the Vampire

After returning a much brighter-spirited Toby to Mr. Sherman, we whistled for a hansom to take us to King's Cross Station. My companion did not instruct the driver to hasten. Why we were proceeding in such a leisurely fashion when so much was at stake remained a mystery to me until Holmes explained that the slightest sign of pursuit would seal Mary's fate.

"Following a suspect," he informed me, "is simple. Any idiot can do it, as those stalwarts at Scotland Yard have demonstrated upon so many occasions. The true art–and the danger–lies in concealing the fact from him that he is being followed. If we were to arrive at the station before Dracula's train has left and he were to spot us, then your wife's life would not be worth a bad florin." He gripped my arm briefly and reassuringly. "Courage, dear fellow. All that can be done is being done."

The third clerk we talked to at the station remembered having sold a ticket to Whitby to a tall stranger with an eerie manner, but expressed no recollection of a woman answering Mary's description in his company. He did recall, however, that the passenger had an oblong box with him which was loaded into the baggage car, and that it took three men to lift it.

"Can you tell us when the next train leaves for Whitby?" Holmes asked the clerk.

He examined his schedule. "There is no direct train to Whitby, sir. But you can catch the first shuttle tomorrow morning at six, if you don't mind an overnight wait between stations. Would you like a ticket?"

"Too late." The detective's expression when we left the window was concerned. "It is as I thought," he said. "He has her shut up in the box."

I shuddered at the thought of that dainty creature forced to share that chamber of death with stale earth from the fiend's accursed homeland. "What now, Holmes?" I demanded. "It is ten o'clock at night. The villain has a head start on us, and we have no way of following."

"On the contrary, Watson," said he, eyes a-twinkle. "Somewhere in this city there is a coachman who can outdrive the fastest train upon the isle. I am speaking of Caesar, who broke all records precipitating us to the spot where we caught Mrs. Harker's train ten miles south of London. With his help we may be in Whitby in time to apprehend Dracula before he leaves the realm."

"But will we be able to find Caesar?"

His face was flushed. "Once I have notified the members of the Baker Street Irregulars," he assured me, "the burden will be upon Caesar to keep himself from being found." And upon that note he struck off in quest of a hansom, forcing me to run in order to catch up.

In an alley near our Baker Street residence we found a number of street Arabs engaged in a game of mumbletypeg with a scarred block of wood and a rusty-bladed knife. The latter was clutched in the dirty fist of a boy I recognised as Simpson, undisputed head of Holmes's private intelligence network. At our appearance he shot to his feet and saluted in a most comical imitation of a soldier at attention, followed in ragged succession by his companions. The result was about as far removed from a military formation as one could get and still make the comparison.

"You're all here then," Holmes observed approvingly. "There's a half-crown coming to the man who finds and brings to my quarters a coachman with long grizzled hair and a battered topper who answers to the name of Caesar. A crown if he's presented within the next thirty minutes. Dismissed."

Six soot-stained hands flew up in a salute that would have made an officer I once knew in the Fifth Northumberland Fusiliers turn purple, and with a scuffle of bare feet the urchins were off in six different directions to do their commander's bidding. Holmes chuckled.

"Good lads, every one of them," he said. "We shall be on our way in no time."

Twenty minutes later we were in my friend's rooms–Holmes sitting, myself pacing the floor–when a four-wheeler rolled to a halt upon the street in front of the building. A diminutive form attired in rags sprang from the rear seat and ran towards the front door.

"It is Simpson!" I cried, snatching up my hat and coat.

Mrs. Hudson, who had postponed retiring in order to brew us a pot of coffee, was engaged in shooing away the slovenly little creature with a broom when we got to the foot of the stairs. Holmes assured her that everything was all right and sent her back inside. "Good work, Simpson." He drew a handful of coins from his coat pocket and dropped them into the lad's cupped hands. "There's a crown for you and a shilling for each of the others. See that they get them."

When Simpson had dashed off with his booty, the detective turned his attention upon the driver seated atop the vehicle. "Good evening, Caesar. Do you remember us?"

Caesar had a cherry-red face which lit up in the dim illumination of the gaslamp above his head when he recognised his passenger of a few days before. "Indeed I do, sir," he replied, nodding boisterously. "H'ain't 'ad the chance ter pull out all the stops like that since I was a lad. Did us good, it did."

"Us?" Holmes raised his eyebrows inquisitively.

The driver inclined his head towards the team in front of him. "Me and the girls, sir. They've been like fillies ever since."

"Would you and the girls care to repeat your performance tonight?"

"Just say the word, sir."

"The word is Whitby."

It was Caesar's turn to raise his eyebrows. "Bless you, sir, but that's a day's hard travel at least. H'ain't quite sure the girls'd be up to it at their advanced age, nor I at mine, truth to tell." He stuck out his lower lip in a doubtful frown.

"Does this make the decision any easier?" Holmes held out his right palm, in which glittered afresh sovereign.

The driver swept up the coin and deposited it in the pocket of his threadbare coat. "'Op in, gentlemen," he said, reaching down to swing open the door of the vehicle.

"This case is costing us, Watson," said Holmes when we were on our way, careening through the fog-laden streets. "But I daresay that the reward of seeing Dracula put out of commission will be sufficient re-imbursement."

I shall not attempt to describe the harrowing journey we took between London and Whitby, other than to say that it aged me considerably. All that night and throughout the next day we travelled, stopping only three times to change horses where Holmes was able to smooth the way among the reluctant owners with silver–"Don't worry, Caesar," he said during the first stop, "we'll pick up your girls on the way home"–and to rest and eat. That Caesar was familiar with the route was obvious, for, despite the fog that had rolled in to cover the entire eastern coast and reduce even the most prominent landmarks to slightly darker shadows in the all-encompassing greyness, he did not miss a turn. Nor, it seemed to me, did he miss a bump among the many that peppered the twisting gravel roads and narrow lanes over which we bounced. By midnight of the second night, October fourth, when we drew near enough to detect the unmistakable fish-and-humanity odour of the seacoast town, I felt as if I had ridden the entire distance on horseback.

"I'm afraid I've muffed it for you, sir," Caesar told us as he let us off in front of the Whitby railway station. "If it wasn't for this blarsted fog, I'd of got you 'ere sooner."

Holmes gripped the driver's callused hand warmly. "Your concern is unnecessary. I think we know where our quarry went from here. Here is another sovereign; get yourself a room for tonight and start back to London in the morning."

Caesar shook his grizzled head, declining the offer. "Keep your money, Mr. 'Olmes. We'll meet you 'ere at eight if you've a mind to go back with us. Good night to you, sirs." He gave his reins a flip and rattled off in the direction of the waterfront hotel.

"What now?" I asked caustically. My mood had not improved during the long and uncomfortable ride from London.

"The shipping offices, Watson," replied the detective. "Someone there should remember a man of Dracula's description booking passage for himself and a large box of earth."

Most of the shipping offices were closed, but in one there was a light, and after pounding upon the door and arguing with the clerk inside for some minutes we succeeded in getting him to open the door. The clerk was a stout creature with a round, balding head and shirtsleeves rolled up to reveal a pair of muscular forearms. One of the eyes glaring at us suspiciously from beneath his thatch-like red brows gleamed most unnaturally; I judged it to be an artificial one of glass.

"The office is closed," he growled. "Come back Monday morning." The door closed with a bang.

Holmes sighed, and, drawing a half-crown from the dwindling supply in his pocket, bent down and proceeded to slide it beneath the door. It acted like a talisman. A moment later the door was opened again and we were greeted with a much friendlier face.

"Come in, gentlemen," said the clerk.

The office was a cramped enclosure in which a battered desk appeared to be the most important furnishing, its top littered with shipping schedules and sheets of figures. A little stove glowed red in one corner, which explained the clerk's rolled-up sleeves, for the atmosphere was stifling. Our host took a squeaking seat in the chair behind the desk and leaned back with his hands clasped behind his neck. "Now what can I do for you two gentlemen?"

Holmes provided him with descriptions of the man we were looking for and his strange cargo and asked the clerk if he had seen him. The latter frowned thoughtfully and sank his pudgy chin onto his chest.

"Don't mean nothing to me," he said. "Just a minute." He leaned back even farther in his chair, and, grasping the sash of the window behind him, wrenched it open with one hand. The noise it made on its way up was sufficient evidence of the tremendous strength in the man's wrists. "Clancy!" he called, in the direction of the wharf. "Come in here, will you?"

There was a muffled reply from outside, and then the window was slammed shut. "Old Clancy's been loadin' cargo off these here docks for forty years," the clerk informed us. "If your man's been here, he's seen him."

Clancy turned out to be a withered salt of indeterminate age whose stringy neck and nearly hairless head protruded from the collar of his pea jacket like the gnarled handle of a walking stick above the top of an umbrella stand. He, too, had a bad eye, but unlike the clerk, he wore no artificial substitute, preferring instead to shade his disfigurement beneath the shiny black peak of the cap he wore upon one side of his head. The picture of the colourful seaman was completed by a lump of tobacco which distorted his right cheek. He closed the door behind him and stood there expectantly, looking from one to the other of us.

Holmes repeated what he had told the clerk and asked the old longshoreman if he had seen the man he described. At first Clancy seemed reluctant to talk, but once the detective had handed him a coin he proved to be as communicative as a seagoing parrot. His reply was so riddled with profanities that I can do little more than paraphrase it in these pages.

It seemed that Clancy had been seated the night before upon a piling engaged in smoking his pipe when a man answering the description Holmes had given him clattered onto the dock in the driver's seat of a waggon and leaped off to enter a rival shipping office. A few moments later he emerged, and, after leading the horses up to the edge of the dock, handed Clancy a gold coin and commanded him to see that the crate on the back of the waggon was loaded onto the *Czarina Catherine*, a sailing ship berthed nearby. Something about the stranger's manner, and particularly his appearance, unnerved the longshoreman, but since the coin appeared to be genuine he put out his pipe and got up to seek some help with the crate. It took three strong men a quarter of an hour to transport the cargo into the hold of the ship, and every step they took was under the stranger's supervision; when, however, the box was securely stowed away and Clancy turned to report the fact to his benefactor, he was nowhere to be found. The longshoreman had still been pondering the sudden nature of the man's disappearance when the clerk called him into the office to speak to us. "Don't seem natural, him just up and vanishin' like that, into thin air, as it war," he concluded.

"What is the *Czarina Catherine*'s destination?" Holmes demanded of the clerk.

The latter shuffled through the papers upon his desk. "Varna, on the coast of the Black Sea," he said at last. "She sails at eight o'clock this morning."

"Varna!" I cried. "Holmes, that was the *Demeter*'s port of arrival!"

"Where is she berthed?" asked Holmes.

"Nearby. Clancy'll take you to her." Curiosity glittered in the clerk's good eye. "What's this fellow wanted for? Smugglin'?"

"In a manner of, speaking." My companion took hold of the old longshoreman's arm and we left the office.

The *Czarina Catherine* rose black among the billows of pale fog wafting landward from the harbour, its archaic sails furled tightly so that its masts and yardarms resembled the skeletal remains of a creature from the dawn of time. Rigging creaked and plank groaned against plank with the ship's restless movement upon the water. I was reminded unpleasantly of the bleak scene aboard the beached *Demeter* at the beginning of the nightmare, and wondered if this unnatural mist accompanied Dracula wherever he went. We left

Clancy upon the dock and approached the gangplank, only to stop when we spotted a broad-shouldered seaman in a greasy pea jacket and high-necked pullover smoking a cigar at its foot.

"He won't look kindly upon a pair of landlubbers invading his ship," Holmes whispered. "Stand by me, Watson; we are going to run a bluff."

Our approach was heard by the sailor, who stepped in front of the gangplank to block our path. "Ship's out of bounds tonight, mates," he said warningly. "Try us again in the morning." He was a big man with a beetling brow and a face the colour of mahogany, among the many seams of which was a number of old scars, evidence of his participation in more than a few brawls aboard ship. His doubled-up fists were like salted hams at his sides.

"Well done, sailor," said Holmes, in a tone of official approval. "The rest of the port authorities shall learn of the vigilance of the *Czarina Catherine*'s crew."

"You're a port authority?" The sailor eyed him suspiciously.

Holmes placed his finger to his lips. "We mustn't alarm the entire harbour," he cautioned him. "A bit of discretion, and none but us will know of the unpleasant duty upon which my colleague and I are engaged."

"You don't look like no port official I ever seen."

"Indeed? And what, pray tell me, does a port official look like?" When the other did not answer, he went on. "If you will but stand aside, we will be able to clear up this most vital business without having to report that a British sailor sought to put a Russian vessel before his own Queen and country. I shudder to think what the popular press would make of that."

This statement had its effect upon the big man, whose stern countenance changed to one of concern, then indignation. "I'll have you know, sir, that I served my time with 'Er Majesty's Navy in India, and that there is no one more loyal to the Jack than Ned Bridger. I ain't no less of an Englishman just because I sail with Rooshans. Just state your business, and you'll see how loyal I am."

Holmes appeared to think it over. Finally he nodded and motioned the sailor closer. "Have you ever heard of the Watson Plan?" he asked in a hushed voice. "No? It comes as no surprise that you have not, for it is probably the most jealously guarded secret to come out of Whitehall within the past ten years." He raised his head and cast a cautious glance in every direction. Apparently satisfied that no one else was within earshot, he went on. "If I did not believe that you were an honest man who would protect his country's secrets with his very life, I would not be telling you this. Once implemented, Professor Watson's brilliant plan for the coastal defence of England would render this isle virtually immune from outside attack for the next thirty years."

Ned Bridger pursed his lips in a silent whistle.

"I see that you are aware of the enormous importance of this operation and of the disastrous consequences which will surely ensue should the plans fall into the wrong hands. As befits its lofty place in the hierarchy of world power, England is a hotbed of spies. We have reason to believe that one of them, a man who goes by the name of Count Dracula, has obtained a copy of the Watson Plan and that he has smuggled it aboard the *Czarina Catherine* preparatory to transporting it to his superiors upon the Continent. We know that he has secreted the voluminous sheafs of papers pertaining to the operation inside a large wooden box of earth, and that he left his hotel late this evening bound for the waterfront. Has any cargo answering this description been carried aboard the *Catherine* during your watch tonight?"

Bridger rubbed his chin thoughtfully. "I've seen nothing of the sort," he replied. Holmes's face fell. "But then, I've only been on duty this last half an hour. Potkin had the watch before that. Your man may have stowed his cargo while he was on duty."

"Do we have your permission to search the ship?"

"I should say you do," said the other, stepping aside from the gangplank. "Nobody'll ever accuse Ned Bridger of standing in the way of his country."

We fled up the gangplank before he could change his mind.

"The 'Watson Plan'?" I whispered to Holmes once we had reached the deck.

"Any port in a storm, Watson," said he. "I did not think that you would mind the temporary promotion. The hold is this way, I believe."

At the top of the ladder which led below hung a lantern, and, once Holmes had lighted it, we experienced little difficulty in locating the cargo storage area. Among the many barrels and crates stacked about the deck was the oblong box for which we were searching. Its casket-like appearance filled me with dread.

"Mary!" I threw myself upon the box and began clawing at the lid with my fingers.

"Let's not lose our heads," Holmes counselled. "There's an easier way." He handed me an iron he found lying atop a nearby tar barrel. Feverishly I inserted the end of it beneath the lid and pried. The boards came away with a groan.

"The lantern, Holmes," I commanded, in a voice tight with suspense. When he lifted it and I saw what the box contained, I uttered a strangled cry.

It was filled with sand.

Chapter Twelve

In Full Cry

I cannot say how long we stood there without moving, staring dumbfounded at the yellowish grains that filled the crate to its top. Eventually my shock gave way to panic. I plunged my hands into the box and clawed through the sand in the insane hope that I would encounter my wife's unconscious form, but succeeded only in baring a portion of the box's plank bottom. Holmes seized my arm in his firm grip.

"She's not here, Watson," he said. "The box is a decoy. We've been tricked."

"But where is she, Holmes?" I was too exhausted emotionally to remove my hands from the box; instead I crouched there with my head hanging, immersed to my elbows in sand. "What has that devil done with Mary?"

He had no answer for that. In the silence that followed my query, the strains of a bawdy sea shanty sung in a voice cracked with age floated in from the direction of the dock. Slowly I raised my head to stare at Holmes.

"Clancy!" we exclaimed in unison, and before the name had a chance to echo in the emptiness of the hold we were stumbling across the deck and clawing for the ladder.

We reached the top deck just in time to lean over the railing and catch sight of a bent figure in a pea jacket shuffling away from the waterfront into the billows of fog that concealed the shipping offices. Below us stood the solid form of Ned Bridger.

"Bridger!" Holmes called out. "Stop that man!" He pointed into the gloom.

There was an agonising moment of delay while the sailor turned to look up at us, and then he was off and running to collar the old longshoreman.

Holmes and I raced down the gangplank, revolvers drawn. We had not gone ten steps along the dock, however, when we heard Bridger's voice calling us. "Over here!" We followed the voice until we came to a row of weather-beaten buildings at the rear of the wharf. Holmes still had the lantern, and as he raised it the light fell upon a welcome sight–that of Clancy pinned against the wall of one of the buildings by Ned Bridger's club-like right arm thrust across his throat.

"He's a game fish, this one is," said the sailor when we were at his side. "Bit me when I tackled him."

"Aye!" cried the longshoreman. "And that ain't all I'd do if I 'ad me prime, ye block-headed, scar-faced hunk of shark bait! Gi' me one second's freedom, and, by Jupiter, I'll–"

"Run away, most likely," finished Holmes, putting away his pistol. "I assure you that such a course will avail you nothing. The man you are protecting, Clancy, is wanted for murder in London. I am sure you would rather assist us than spend what little time remains to you locked up in gaol. Where is Count Dracula, and how much did he pay you to switch boxes?"

The old man said nothing, his good eye glaring defiance.

Holmes sighed. "Very well, if that is the way you prefer it. Watson, summon the police."

I withdrew to obey his instructions.

"'Old it, mate." Clancy's tone was defeated. I stopped and turned. His eye was downcast and there was no longer any sign of opposition upon his weathered countenance. "I'll tell ye what ye wants to know, but first ye got ter call off yer gorilla."

Holmes nodded to Bridger, who reluctantly withdrew his arm. Clancy stood there unmoving, staring at the ground. At length he took a deep breath and commenced his narrative.

"The guv'nor gi' me an extry gold piece ter transfer the contents of the box 'e 'ad with 'im ter an empty crate what was a-layin' on the dock, and ter fill the first wi' sand from the beach," he explained. "I borried a wheelbarrer ter do this, and a spade. By the time I got back wi' a load of sand, the other box war already gone. When the first box is filled, the guv'nor tells me ter load it onto the *Catherine*, and that's when I gets the three blokes ter 'elp me. The rest I told you before."

"What sort of creature would agree to help another in the abduction of an innocent woman for a mere piece of gold?" I demanded.

The longshoreman's eye widened with astonishment. "What kind of bilge do ye take me fer, mate?" he said indignantly. "There warn't no woman with 'im, abducted or otherwise."

"He didn't have her in the box?" Holmes pressed.

"There warn't nothin' in the box but dirt. I've knowed me share of females from 'ere to Singapore, guv, and any one of 'em can tell ye there h'ain't nobody 'as more respect for woman'ood than old Clancy."

"What can this mean, Holmes?" I felt weak. Had he disposed of her along the way? I was afraid to put the question into words.

"Steady, Watson." He fixed Clancy with his piercing gaze. "Where is the second box?"

The dock worker shrugged. "Search me, mate. Like I told ye, it war gone when I got back wi' the sand."

Holmes swung his attention upon Ned Bridger. "What ships have left this harbour within the last hour?"

"Two, I think," said the other, stroking his shadowed chin. "I heard a steamer blowing its whistle half an hour ago, and I helped an American clipper cast off a bit before that. They must both have been overdue, else they wouldn't have left till the fog lifted."

"What do you know about these vessels?" Holmes inquired of Clancy.

"Steamer'd be the *King 'Enry,* bound for Australia." The longshoreman's face was puckered in thought. "Can't say about the other."

"I spoke to her master," Bridger put in. "She's the *Baltimore,* a trader out of Boston."

Holmes told Clancy he could go, and the latter shuffled away before Holmes could change his mind. Now we were alone on the dock with Ned Bridger.

"Where is my wife?" I asked my friend. My manner was so dangerously calm that he stared at me in concern. I think he realised then how close I was to losing my reason.

"The mesmeric powers of the vampire are nearly without limit, as you know only too well," he replied placatingly. "It is likely that Dracula commanded her to remain out of sight until he had concluded his business with Clancy." He clearly wanted to say something more, but decided against it and turned to the big sailor. "Where can we hire a motor launch?"

Bridger's face was a mask of distrust. "Who are you?" he demanded. "And don't tell me again you're with the port authority. I heard enough to know you was diddling me with all that bilge about government plans and foreign spies. I've a good mind to call for a coastguard and have you both clapped in irons. Who's this bloke you're after, and what's he to do with you?"

There was no way around it other than to explain. Quickly Holmes told the sailor our names and drew a sketchy account of our hunt for Count Dracula, leaving out the incredible fact of his vampire existence and concentrating upon his role as a murderer and kidnapper. By the time he finished, Bridger's suspicion had fled and his features were transformed into a captivating smile that was most puzzling under the circumstances.

"You are Sherlock Holmes?" When Holmes assured him that he was, the seaman seized the detective's right hand and began pumping it with such energy that it seemed he was attempting to pull it off. "I've been waiting a long time to meet you, Mr. Holmes," he said boisterously. "Surely you remember my brother Morgan, who was skipper of the *Alicia* when it sailed into that patch of fog in the Channel two years ago?"

"From which it never emerged," nodded Holmes, wincing either from the pressure of Bridger's hand or from the memory of that unsatisfactory case. "Your gratitude is misplaced, I fear. The disappearance of the *Alicia* is one problem I was never able to solve."

"But you proved from my brother's record that the fate of his vessel could not have been due to any error upon his part, as the authorities attempted to claim. For that I will always be indebted to you."

"You are too kind. At present, however, we are still in need of a boat."

The sailor favoured us both with a broad wink. "I know of a steam launch moored near here, whose owner would never be the wiser if we borrowed it tonight."

"Excellent! Now, if you would kindly release your grip upon my hand and lead us to the vessel in question, we would be delighted to accompany you. Make haste, my dear fellow! The *Baltimore* has too much of a head start upon us now."

"Why not the *King Henry*?" I asked my companion as we strode along the dock in the sailor's wake.

He shook his head. "The distance to Australia is too great. Considering Dracula's appetite, he would run out of crew members long before he reached port. No, Watson, he is on his way to the conquest of the United States of America, and all the arrangements involving the *Czarina Catherine* were merely part of an elaborate device to throw us off the track. He nearly succeeded."

There proved to be ample fuel aboard the diminutive steamer, and after what seemed an eternity, but which by my watch was scarcely more than a quarter of an hour, Ned Bridger succeeded in getting the engine into operation. At Holmes's insistence I took control of the tiller while he stood in the bow. With the exception of the boiler clattering and clanking and belching steam in the centre of the vessel, the scene was reminiscent of Leutze's famous painting of George Washington crossing the Delaware, with an extremely lanky and hawk-like General Washington in command.

"No lights, please," said Holmes when Bridger leaned forward to ignite the running-lamp hanging over the side in front. The latter stared up at him incredulously.

"In this muck?" he protested. "That'd be suicide!"

"It's either that or murder, which would certainly be Mrs. Watson's fate if Dracula spotted us following. I leave the choice to you."

"For God's sake, Bridger, let it be," I cried.

Grudgingly the sailor put out his vesta and cast off the lines. A moment later we eased out into the lampblack gloom of the harbour.

The fog, which had parted sluggishly to allow us entrance, soon closed in about us until we seemed to be floating through eternal night. The famous London mists with which I was so familiar bore little resemblance to this insidious, choking mass, the very density of which made breathing difficult, and I began to wonder if it were not a creation of Dracula's meant to discourage pursuit. I was reminded of Van Helsing's claim that the vampire was capable of controlling the weather within his immediate vicinity. If so, and if this impenetrable vapour owed its origins to the supernatural, then we were closer to our quarry than I had dared hope.

"Starboard a bit on that rudder, Doctor." Bridger's voice was reassuringly solid above the powerful thrum of the engine. "If our bird expects to reach the open sea, he's got to miss that reef first."

How long we spent groping our way through that harbour I cannot even begin to guess. My watch was useless in the gloom. Once or twice I thought I detected the muffled chime of church bells striking the hour, but it was difficult to distinguish them from the metallic noises the engine was making, so that I could not count them nor even be sure that I had heard them at all. After a while it was hard to imagine that there was any world beyond this one of cold and darkness. Under these conditions fatigue and concern for my wife's safety soon took their toll of me, and I think that I had begun to doze when Holmes's excited exclamation brought me back to reality with a jolt.

"Halloa!"

"What is it, Holmes? Did you see something?"

"I am not sure." He was an indistinct shadow in the bow of the launch, scarcely distinguishable from the cylindrical boiler which separated us. "It appeared to be a light, but it may have been only the North Star breaking through the cloud cover."

For an agonising moment we remained silent, straining our eyes in an attempt to penetrate the billows of fog rolling past the bow. When nothing materialised, my heart sank into my boots. Was Dracula to succeed? My apprehensions had turned in this dismal direction when suddenly I saw it too.

"Holmes!" I cried. "There it is! Off the port bow!"

It was a pinpoint of yellow, glowing unmistakably against a backdrop of midnight black and seeming to hover in mid air some six hundred yards ahead of us and to our left. From time to time it would vanish as a fresh plume of fog scudded before our view, only to return bold as ever as soon as the obstruction was past. To me it was a beacon of hope at the end of a long and grievous journey.

"That's the light on the fo'c'sle, or I'm a landlubber," said Bridger.

"Full speed ahead, Bridger," commanded Holmes in his high-pitched voice. "Overtake her."

"I'll do what I can, but if we fetch up on that reef, it's a watery grave for us all." So saying, the sailor opened the throttle and we shot forward with a jolt that nearly sent me tumbling over the stern. "Hard starboard on that tiller!" he shouted over the din.

I did as directed. The bow swung in the direction of the light, cleaving across the surface at a blinding rate of speed and dousing us all with ice-cold spray. The wind of our passage lashed at my face, numbing my cheeks. My hat was lifted from my head and sent bouncing into our wake. I made no attempt to catch it. Ahead of us the light loomed closer with each passing second.

I doubt that in the excitement of the moment it occurred to any of us what we would do once we overtook the clipper. Boarding her would have been ridiculous without the consent of her captain, and the chances of obtaining that consent under the present circumstances were improbable at best. It was likely that such a manoeuvre would result in our being clapped in irons immediately upon reaching the deck. At any rate, however, those considerations could wait until we had succeeded in catching up with the vessel. Our main concern at the moment was one of speed and how to get it out of the throbbing engine without actually bursting the boiler.

We were within a thousand feet of the *Baltimore* when the light toward which we were racing ceased to draw closer. For a long moment it hovered there motionless, and then, gradually, it began to move away. I felt a sinking sensation at the pit of my stomach.

"It's getting away!" I moaned.

Holmes cursed, a thing I had rarely known him to do. "He's spotted us, blast it! I forgot he can see in the dark. The captain and crew must be under his control. More speed, Bridger! Throw on more fuel!"

"Impossible! The boiler's about to go up like a blinking Roman candle now!"

"More speed, I say!"

"All right! Meet you in Hell!" The sailor threw a shovelful of coal into the firebox and pushed the throttle forward all the way. The pistons responded with a roar and we bounced across the water like a flat stone.

The fog was beginning to dissipate, a development in which I rejoiced until I realised that this was because of the mounting wind. It filled the clipper's voluminous sails, now visible against the leaden sky, and pushed it along with a speed our modern proponents of steam power would not have deemed possible in such an outmoded vessel. Our boiler was strained to its bursting point just in order for us to maintain the same rate of travel. I am not one to blame human misfortunes upon the elements, and yet I could do naught but suspect that such a wind, so favourable to our quarry, could have only supernatural origins. Nevertheless, we stuck to the clipper's stern with a pertinacity that would have made the tracker-dog Toby proud.

"Faster, Bridger!" cried Holmes. "We're doing no more than holding our own!"

"I can't scoop coal and man the throttle at the same time!"

Holmes tore off his coat and hastened to Bridger's side, where he took up the shovel and fell to scooping coal into the firebox with the feverish energy that was his alone.

A great deafening peal of thunder uncurled itself over our heads, sounding for all the world like an enormous whip being wielded by some unearthly hand. Immediately the clouds opened up and released a torrent of water down upon our heads. Lightning streaked the sky. Waves leaped over the bow of the launch and dashed themselves against the deck. The phenomenon was too sudden, and too amicable to our opponent's cause, to be attributed to the realm of coincidence; Dracula was calling upon all his powers to elude us.

"Mind the firebox!" the sailor warned Holmes. Indeed, the water sloshing about the deck was threatening to extinguish the flames to which we owed our progress. I had a terrible vision of our vessel drifting dead in the water among these hostile seas while the *Baltimore* continued on its way unencumbered. The detective paid no heed as he proceeded to shovel more fuel into the greedy flames.

The boiler began to chatter and shake until the entire vessel was oscillating from bow to stern. I had all I could do to maintain my grip upon the tiller, so violently had it begun to vibrate in my hand.

"She's going to blow!" shouted Bridger.

For the first time since he had taken up the shovel, Holmes ceased his ministrations and stood leaning upon the instrument. "Keep your hand on that throttle!" he commanded the seaman, who had been about to let go of it. Bridger stared at him strangely.

"Blimey," he said, barely loud enough to make himself heard over the din of the engine and the storm. "You're mad as a gull!"

"How good a swimmer are you, Bridger?" Holmes asked.

"What?"

"Can you swim to shore from here?"

"I've swum farther," he responded, still not catching the other's drift.

"Then let me have the throttle and you jump overboard. Watson and I will take it from here."

At last the sailor understood. He thrust out his jaw. "Are you calling me a coward?"

"Not at all. But this is not your fight. There is no sense in your taking further risks."

"This boat is my responsibility. I'll not turn it over to any landlubber."

"Don't be a fool, Bridger!" Holmes exclaimed. "You have nothing to gain by these heroics."

"Sorry, mate. Can't hear you." He chewed on the stub of his cigar, which had long since gone out, and returned his attention to the clipper's retreating stern. The throttle shuddered uncontrollably in his strong left hand.

"Holmes! Look!" I rose to my feet and pointed out past the bow. The wind, which until now had been blowing out to sea, had taken a sudden half-turn, sweeping the *Baltimore* perpendicular to our line of view and precipitating it towards the southern end of the harbour. Holmes eyed this development with the air of a hunter watching a fleeing fox.

"He's dodging; trying to lose us."

"He'll lose more than that if he don't turn soon," remarked Bridger. "He's heading straight for the reef."

We watched in silence as the vessel continued upon its path of self-destruction. My thoughts were of Mary. Had the fiend decided to sacrifice everything, including her, in order to make good his escape? No, it was more likely that he was unaware of the reef's existence and was taking this action in the hopes of forcing us to overload our already swollen boiler. In either case, my helpmate's life was in danger. My knuckles turned white, so tightly did I grip the tiller in my frustration. To be forced to stand by helplessly and watch one's entire world rushing headlong towards calamity is a descent into deepest Hell.

There was a flash of lightning, and in its illumination I thought I glimpsed something fall off the stern of the clipper and disappear into the black waters. "What's that?" I inquired of my companions. I had barely got the question out when there was another flash and I saw more objects leaving the deck of the doomed ship. I felt sick inside.

"Good lord," I whispered. "Those are men."

"No doubt they prefer the ocean to the horns of the reef," Holmes observed, indicating the waters to the south. There the shimmering whiteness of the reef lay exposed where the wind was whipping the waves into a fine spray. I was reminded of the fangs of the hound of the Baskervilles, not to mention those of the Bloofer Lady and of Dracula himself, which were no less white and no less deadly.

The boiler began to hiss ominously, the sound increasing in volume and intensity with each passing second. "*There she goes!*" Bridger shouted.

"Into the water, Watson," said Holmes. His voice was icily calm, a feature it took on only when the situation was most urgent.

I hesitated, wondering if my left arm, the shoulder of which had been shattered by a Jezail bullet at the battle of Maiwand when I was with the Army Medical Department, was up to the task. My mind was made up for me when Holmes hooked his right leg around my ankle, and, with the aid of his hip, swept me off my feet and over the side. I hit the water head first.

The water was cold as death, but that was hardly my first concern. For a long time I kept travelling downward, and with a rush of panic I began to fear that I would never return to the surface. At length, however, my progress slowed; I began kicking and flailing my way back to the world of light and life, with no thought of the discomfort this exertion was causing my wounded shoulder. After what seemed an eternity I broke the surface and gulped in great mouthfuls of sweet air. I shucked off my ulster, the weight of which had been increased twofold as a result of its soaking, and after retrieving my revolver from its pocket, consigned it to the harbour's murky depths. Thus relieved of its burden, I found that I was able to keep my head above the icy water with little effort.

There was a tremendous explosion to my left, and as if illuminated by one of the lightning flashes that continued to split the sky, the harbour was thrown into blazing brightness. When I swung my head in that direction all I could see was a pillar of blinding flame rising straight up from the surface of the water and towering against the charcoal-grey clouds. Debris splashed down all around me. In my confused state it took me a moment to recognise the fragments as belonging to the steam launch I had recently vacated.

My first thought was of Holmes. Had he, too, succeeded in quitting the craft before the boiler burst? Or could this be his funeral pyre, lighting up the sky as he himself had seemed to do so often with the revelations of his remarkable brain? I opened my mouth and shouted his name at the top of my lungs.

"Holmes!"

There was no reply, just the thunder and the howling of the wind. I tried a second and a third time. Nothing. This, then, was how it ended. All the deductions, all the hours spent poring over clues and following the trails left by criminals throughout England and the Continent, all the telegrams from the powerful and the destitute requesting the master detective's aid in solving mysteries of the densest nature, all the rewards offered and declined–all had come to nothing more than an icy grave in a remote English harbour. It was with lead in my heart that I turned away from the crackling wreckage of the launch and began swimming towards shore.

Unlike my friend, who despite his distaste for exercise for its own sake had been able to maintain his fighting trim through all the days of his life, I was far from being in condition. My shoulder began to ache terribly before I had swum even half the distance that stretched between myself and dry land, and I had trouble getting my breath. If not for the happy circumstance that a tongue of sand had accumulated upon the solid foundation of the reef, I have no illusions but that I would have succumbed to fatigue and cold and drowned long before reaching safety. As it was, I found myself barely able to crawl far enough onto the bar to keep from sliding back into the water the moment I lost consciousness, which I proceeded to do immediately upon accomplishing this all-important task.

I could not have been senseless for long, because when I came around, I could still see what was left of the launch blazing brightly in the harbour. And I saw something else as well.

I saw the *Baltimore* perched not twenty feet from where I was lying.

There was a great gaping hole in the bow where it had struck the reef on its way to the sand bar, but other than that, the vessel appeared to be unharmed. Indeed, even the damage that had been done, fatal enough in the water, was rendered ineffectual by the fact that the entire front half of the vessel was clear of the sea, its prow stabbing heavenward. The loosened rigging hung in tangles all about the deck.

My relief upon spotting this evidence that my wife may not have perished was tempered by a sobering thought: where was Dracula? In the next instant my question was answered, for a jagged streak of lightning illuminated the scene and I saw the fiend standing upon the forecastle.

He was staring down at me, his red eyes glowing fiercely amidst the pallor of his features. His black cloak flapped like bats' wings in the gale-force wind. He was holding something in his arms; I had hardly to look to recognise the limp form in the white night-dress as that of my Mary. Whether she was alive or dead was something I could not tell at that distance. If it were the latter, then I was prepared–nay, determined–to sacrifice my own life, as had Holmes, if in so doing I could bring an end to this vile creature's existence.

For a long moment we stood motionless, glaring at each other across the score of feet that separated us. Then Dracula turned and disappeared into the captain's cabin. That I had been challenged to follow was a certainty.

I felt a chill that had nothing to do with the temperature or my own soaked condition. Sherlock Holmes was dead, and I was alone against Count Dracula.

Chapter Thirteen

Confrontation

I was still standing there long after the lightning had ceased, and the scene was draped in midnight black once again. To claim that I was not afraid would be to strain my readers' gullibility to the breaking point; nevertheless, it was not fear for myself that made me hesitate, but rather the fear that I would walk into Dracula's trap and die without avenging the deaths of Holmes and Bridger and the abduction of my wife. To perish was not so much a thing to be avoided as to perish in vain. How I wished that my friend were here now! He alone would know how best to approach the situation. He had not been gone half an hour, and already his genius was sorely missed.

This was gaining me nothing. Sighing, I struck off towards the beached vessel in search of the best way to board her without being observed by the vampire.

I had crept stealthily into the shadows upon the clipper's far side when I was suddenly grabbed from behind and thrown to the ground. When I attempted to cry out a hand was clamped firmly over my mouth. Frantically I struggled to escape, but the fiend's grip proved unbreakable. I was on the verge of resigning myself to eternal damnation when I heard a familiar voice at my ear.

"The slightest sound would prove disastrous to our plans."

It was Holmes! So overcome was I with joy that I think I would have uttered an exclamation of relief had it not been for his hand covering the lower half of my face. Slowly he removed it, at the same time releasing his grip upon my arms so that I was allowed to sit up.

"Holmes!" I whispered, putting out a hand to touch him to make sure I was not dreaming. His shoulder seemed solid enough; although it was wet. His face was featureless in the darkness. "What miracle is this? How is it that you survived that terrible explosion?"

He chuckled softly, a sound I had thought I would never hear again in this world. "Dear Watson," he said quietly. "Only your nature could remain inquisitive in a circumstance such as this. Surviving that terrible explosion was not so difficult as you might think, for the very simple reason that I was not there when it occurred."

"You were not there?"

"No, Watson, I was not there. Remaining aboard a vessel which is about to be blown to kingdom come is not among the many idiosyncrasies which you have been faithful enough to catalogue in your accounts of my character. I jumped."

"Wonderful! But where is Bridger? Is he with you?"

There was a long pause before he responded. "No, Watson, he is not."

I felt suddenly empty. "Do you mean–?"

"I jumped with Bridger's assurance that he would be right behind me. Whether he was telling the truth or not is a moot point, since the boiler blew just as I hit the water. He did not have time to jump."

"He was a brave man," I said after a moment.

"The question of his bravery is hardly an important one now that he is dead," said my friend, rather callously, I thought. "It is up to us to see that he did not die in vain. You saw Dracula a few moments ago?"

It took me a second to react after the seeming insensitivity of his earlier statement. Finally I nodded. "Yes. He has Mary with him."

"So I observed. Under the Count's manipulation she appears to have exchanged her role as hostage for another one as bait. I am dead, or so he thinks, and he has so far underestimated your intelligence as to believe he can lure you into a trap. You will, of course, not disappoint him."

"What do you mean?"

I thought I saw the steely glint in his eyes when he turned his head, catching the reflection of the stars which were just beginning to show through a break in the clouds. "Is your watch working? " he inquired.

I drew the instrument out of the pocket of my soaked waistcoat and put it to my ear. "It is ticking."

"I have two minutes of six o'clock." He was studying his own watch in the pale light of those same stars.

"I have the same."

"Good. I will give you five minutes. Enter the hold through the aperture in the bow–Dracula will not be expecting that, it is too obvious–and wait till three minutes after six. At that time you will hear a number of gunshots outside; pay them no attention. Ascend to the deck and make your way to the captain's cabin, where you will find your wife waiting for you. When you have her, shout it out for all the world to hear. Then make for dry land as fast as your legs will carry you. I don't have to remind you that Mrs. Watson's life as well as your own depends upon the speed you will be making."

"And what will you be doing all this time?" I asked him.

He slid his revolver from the pocket of his waterproof Inverness. It looked comparatively dry. "I will be doing something with which the

Count will no doubt be familiar from his experience upon the field of battle, but which I am gambling he will not be expecting in this instance. I am going to create a diversion."

"You've charted yourself a dangerous course," I warned him.

"One hour at sea and already your speech is becoming nautical," he mused. "Seriously, it is not half so dangerous as the one I've assigned you. Considering your relationship to the lady involved, however, I thought that you would rather be the one who came to her rescue. But climb upon your bicycle, Watson; we've wasted one of your allotted five minutes already." So saying, he melted back into the shadows and was gone.

Climbing through the hole in the clipper's bow was not as easy as it sounded. It was tilted more than six feet off the ground, and I was forced to stand on tiptoe and stretch my arms as high as they would go in order to get a grip upon the bottom edge of the aperture and haul myself inside. I cannot begin to describe the agony this caused for my already aching shoulder. The pain was nullified, however, by the thought of the anguish I knew would be mine for the rest of my life if I let it stand in the way of freeing my Mary from the fiend's grasp.

I landed silently upon my feet inside the hold. At first it seemed quite black, but as my eyes grew accustomed to the poor light, I saw the reflected illumination of starlight coming through the opened hatch and shimmering upon the surface of the water that had collected aft of the bow. I took out my watch and turned its face to catch the light. One minute after six. Cautiously I picked my way down the tilted deck–it was wet and slippery–towards the wooden ladder that led into the open, there to await Holmes's signal.

He was right on time. At 6.03, two gunshots sounded outside, and I lost no time in clambering up the ladder. My alacrity nearly cost me my life.

No sooner had I reached the top deck than I felt a sudden chill, such as is caused by the rush of cold air when someone opens the door in a warm room in the dead of winter. I had experienced that same sensation enough times not to have to think about it. Immediately I dove for the nearest shadow. I had not moved a second too soon, for when I peered out from my sanctuary in the darkened section between the captain's cabin and the starboard railing, I saw a black-cloaked figure hasten past within touching distance of my hand. When I say "within touching distance," I am of course speaking figuratively, for I felt no desire to make physical contact with the waxen flesh of the Vampire King as he made his way to the bow, from which direction the shots had come.

I don't have to remind you that Mrs. Watson's life as well as your own will depend upon the speed you will be making, Holmes had said. I followed his advice and ducked in through the doorway of the cabin as soon as Dracula's back was towards me.

After descending a short ladder, I found myself inside a windowless enclosure which no light penetrated. I fumbled around until I located a lantern hanging upon a hook beside the entrance, and after two of the vestas I had taken from the damp inside pocket of my jacket failed, succeeded in igniting a third and lit the wick. A dim glow blossomed in the darkness of the cabin. I peered anxiously through the gloom, and there was Mary.

Those who have read my description of the lady who was to become my wife in "The Sign of Four"–blond, dainty, firm of step and careful of dress–would not have recognised the woman who sat motionless in the straight-backed chair in the centre of the cabin. To begin with, her coiffure, not a hair of which I had ever known to be out of place since we had met, had come loose and now flowed unfettered about her white shoulders. She had lost her robe and slippers; shivering in the gossamer stuff of her night-dress, she looked very frail indeed, like a baby bird that had tumbled from its nest. Her blue eyes were wide–not with terror, as I had expected them to be, coming upon her so suddenly when she must virtually have given up hope of ever being rescued–but with unseeing stupor. I recognised the signs of hypnosis. Holmes had been right when he had surmised that Dracula had put her in a mesmeric trance in order to prevent her escape. My first act, after falling upon her and embracing her from sheer relief, was to examine her throat for punctures. There were none. Thanking God for delivering her from that horror, I wrapped her in a coarse woollen blanket taken from the cabin bunk, gathered her into my arms, and carried her to the deck.

Dracula was speaking when I got to the top of the steps. The sound of that resonant voice, which seemed neither to increase nor diminish in volume whether one was drawing towards or away from its source, filled me with hatred and dread. In its vibrance I seemed to detect the rustle of grave-worms amidst red satin and the sharp odour of freshly turned earth.

"So you live still," said the voice.

I started at the words, nearly dropping my frail burden, but when I looked around there was no sign of the vampire on board of the clipper. Then I heard Holmes's shrill tones in reply, and I knew that it was he whom Dracula had been addressing.

"Did you think I would go to my grave and leave you here to prey upon whom you please?" The detective was standing upon the very edge of the sand bar, having worked his way towards the stern of the clipper. Between him and the beached ship stood Count Dracula with his back towards me. I saw the movement of his heavy cloak in the chill wind.

"Where is your companion?"

That was my cue. "I have her, Holmes!" I shouted over the gale.

Dracula swung about with the speed of a panther caught between two marksmen. His expression when he saw me with his hostage was savage.

"Run, Watson, run!" In three leaps Sherlock Holmes succeeded in thrusting himself between the Count and the *Baltimore.* It was the bravest deed I have ever witnessed, my friend placing himself in the fiend's path and brandishing his pistol as if it could be of any use against so impregnable a foe that I might escape. I was so caught up in this spectacle that I did not give a thought to the welfare either of my wife or myself, and instead of running I remained rooted before the entrance to the captain's cabin. Dracula laughed.

"Fire your pitiable weapon, Sherlock Holmes," he taunted. "See what good it will do you against a man who commanded armies hundreds of years before you were born."

Holmes fired, once, twice, thrice. He kept squeezing the trigger until the hammer clicked against an empty cylinder. When the smoke cleared the vampire was still standing. His laugh was hideous. He swept Holmes aside, as at the slaughter-house, with an indifferent arm and began climbing up the side of the vessel, upon which I was standing, in the manner of a lizard scaling a craggy rock.

"Run, Watson!" Holmes cried again, scrambling to his feet. "As you value your life, flee!"

At last, with the fiend less than two yards away, the import of my friend's words struck home. I was on the point of leaping over the side, Mary and all, when I locked glances with Dracula–and froze.

"Mind his eyes! Their gaze is death!"

Perspiration broke out upon my forehead. All of my senses remained intact; I was aware of the senseless woman in my arms, aware of the icy wind ruffling my hair and flapping my coattails, aware of the danger we both were in; but I could not move. Dracula swung a leg over the railing and drew himself silently onto the deck. He was smirking beneath his moustache. He had won. His eyes were twin pools of molten fire towards which I was drawn as inexorably as was a moth to a flame, knowing all the time of the doom that awaited it, but unable to draw back. He was near now, very near; I could smell the rankness of his breath when he bared his fangs.

And then a curious thing happened.

He was near enough so that I could feel his hot breath upon my face, when suddenly there was a change in his eyes. Their shift of emphasis was almost a tangible thing as they left my own burning orbs and slid towards something beyond my shoulder. Then something new came into them, something I had not seen before. It was fear.

If this new development had not been enough to break the spell the vampire had placed over me, it was thoroughly shattered by the sound of Holmes's triumphant voice at his back.

"Beware the sun, Count Dracula," he was saying. "It will sap your strength as surely as did the shears of Samson's Delilah."

I risked a quick glance behind me. True to the detective's word, the first pink rays of sunrise had begun to show upon the horizon, intensifying as the storm clouds retreated before them. The sight of them flooded me with ecstasy; I had given up hope of ever seeing them again.

Dracula hissed and drew his cloak before his face, backing away towards the railing.

"Witness its purifying rays, Count Dracula." The detective was taunting him. "Soon they will reach the ship, and then your power will cease to be. That is when we will destroy you."

The Count could stand it no longer. With a roar of mixed anguish and frustration, he dashed past me–I had barely time to leap out of the way–and bounded cat-like over the clipper's lofty prow. It may have been an optical illusion brought on by my own confusion and abetted by the poor light, but it seemed to me that by the time he landed upon the beach Dracula's outward form resembled nothing so much as an enormous wolf. If this was so, and he had indeed transformed himself, then his powers were already abandoning him, because by the time he came into view again in a moonlight-striped section of beach at the other end of the sand bar, it was a man-like figure I saw fleeing away, his cloak flying behind him. In another moment he was enveloped in shadow for the last time.

"Are you all right, old man?" Holmes was standing beside me now upon the deck.

I nodded. "We must get Mary to a hospital," I said.

"He has harmed her?" There was alarm in his voice. I hastened to reassure him.

"He has not had that chance, thanks to you. But she is in a trance and suffering from exposure. I am concerned about the possibilities of pneumonia."

"Then, by all means, let us–but what's this?"

He was gazing beyond my shoulder in the direction from which the sun was rising. I turned, and in the instant of doing so beheld a four-wheeled conveyance rattling in our direction over the spot in which I had last seen Count Dracula's retreating form. It was being drawn by a team of powerful horses and its driver was a standing figure in a wildly flapping cloak and tall beaver hat. He was lashing a whip over the beasts' head for speed. My blood turned to ice. Was this some new subterfuge upon the part of the vampire?

He had reined to a swinging halt within a stone's throw of the stranded vessel before I caught sight of the cherry-red colour of his face. My heart soared.

"Holmes!" I cried in relief. "It's Caesar!"

"So it is. Come, Watson."

Together we made our way to ground level, where the driver of the four-wheeler awaited us. The sight of the unconscious woman I held in my arms puzzled him for an instant, but the bewildered expression upon his countenance soon gave way to joy when he saw that we were both unharmed.

"Blimey!" he said. "When I eard that big blow in the 'arbour, I knowed it 'ad to be you two, and I was just as sure you'd both been blarsted to pieces. Wind bein' what it is, I figured I'd find your corpses washed up 'ere. Where to this time, guv'nors?" He mounted the driver's seat and took up his reins expectantly.

Holmes laughed. "Caesar," he said, "you are a public servant after my own heart." Then he grew sad. "There seems little enough we can do for those poor fellows from the *Baltimore*... Whitby Hospital, my dear fellow, and don't spare the steam." He opened the door of the vehicle for me to enter it with my helpless burden and followed me inside just as we began rolling.

"What about Dracula?" I asked the detective, who had taken the seat opposite. "You are not going to let him get away!"

"Steady, Watson. His ship does not sail for an hour and a half; in the meantime, knowing as I do the propensity of the British hospital director to treat every patient as if he had all the time in the world, I think that my services will be most needed at our destination." He settled back to watch the scenery race past.

The sun was a vengeful red ball upon the horizon.

Chapter Fourteen

End of the Adventure

"I am afraid that I shall have to leave you for a while, Watson," said Sherlock Holmes, when we were both standing in the tiny waiting room of the hospital in Whitby.

I had finished one of the cigars which an orderly had been kind enough to send out for and was engaged in lighting a second from the stub of the first. I paused, staring at him through the thick smoke.

"Are you not going to wait for word of Mary's condition?"

"It seems that you are never satisfied. Half an hour ago you wondered why I did not abandon you so that I could pursue Count Dracula. Now, when I propose to do just that, you ask me to stay. According to the clock on that wall, which by my watch is approximately one minute and forty seconds slow, I have less than seventy-five minutes in which to return to the docks and settle the vampire's hash for good. I pray that Mrs. Watson will be out of danger by the time I return."

I put out my second cigar in a nearby ash tray. "I am going with you," I said.

He shook his head. "You would be worse than useless with your wife hovering between life and death. Besides, what will she think when she awakes and you are not there? She would then be justified in refusing to allow you to accompany me upon any further problems which may come my way. No, Watson, you owe it to your readers as well as to yourself to remain here." He seemed about to say something more, but instead he gripped my hand firmly and met my gaze with an expression of friendship in his eyes such as I had not witnessed before. Then he turned and vanished through the swinging door that led to the lobby and out.

I regretted his departure almost immediately; it was bad enough having to remain idle because my assistance had been politely but firmly refused by the physician in charge, without having to wait alone. The hour hand of the wall clock had made a complete circuit and I had smoked the last of my cigars when the door opened again and in stepped the thick-set, bearded doctor into whose care I had surrendered my wife. I fairly leapt across the room to meet him.

"She is resting peacefully," he said in answer to my unspoken question. "She is not out of danger yet, but the worst part of the crisis is past." He was perspiring, despite the coolness of the season.

"May I see her?"

"Yes, but only for a few minutes."

The shades were drawn in the hospital room, striping the bed in which my wife was resting in grey light. She looked extremely small and fragile against the white sheet and voluminous pillow. As I approached she opened her eyes and smiled.

"I knew it was you as soon as I heard your footsteps," she said weakly. "I am something of a detective myself, you see."

I was unable to reply. Kneeling beside the bed, I took her hand in both of mine and pressed it to my cheek. Her smile deepened and then her eyes closed again. In a moment her even breathing told me she was asleep.

For a long time I remained upon my knees with her little hand sandwiched between my palms, silently expressing my gratitude to God for His mercy. A white-coated intern came in to examine the patient's pulse and adjust the window shades, taking care not to disturb me. I paid him no mind.

"You look as if you could use a bed yourself, Dr. Watson."

I sprang to my feet, my heart pounding. That hellish voice was the last thing I'd expected to hear in this sanctuary. Count Dracula, his complexion nearly as pale as the hospital gown he had drawn on over his black suit, smiled diabolically down at me from his position at the foot of the bed.

"You, here! In broad daylight!" I threw myself in front of him to protect Mary, who was still sleeping soundly, and tore my revolver from the deep pocket of my jacket. He made no move to stop me.

"And why not?" he said. "The sun is not harmful to me; it merely deprives me of the special advantages which I enjoy when it is not present. Why else would I resort to a disguise in order to gain admittance to this chamber, when you have seen for yourself the impossibility of anything standing in my path during the hours of darkness? You may as well put away your weapon, for it is still quite useless against me no matter what the hour." When I did not follow his advice, his expression became grim. "Fear not for your wife. I have not come to do mischief."

"Then why are you here?" I demanded. "And where is Holmes?"

He shrugged, a sinister movement of his right shoulder. "Very near, I fancy. His powers are far in advance of his mortal status. I have little doubt but that he has already pieced together my movements since leaving the waterfront and is on his way here even now. My time draws short. My business will not take more than a moment."

"And what is your business?"

"Curiosity, Dr. Watson." He fixed me with his terrible eyes, but this time there was something wrong about them. I had seen them reflect a variety of emotions, from blind rage to triumph and finally fear, but this was something new. It was more than defeat; I had the distinct impression that I was gazing into a well of unfathomable sorrow.

"Curiosity?" I echoed.

"I can understand Professor Van Helsing's motives in wishing to destroy me. Nor is there mystery in Jonathan Harker's and Arthur Holmwood's decisions to accompany him in this task, for both have known tragedy at my hands. To Sherlock Holmes I am a challenge, and I have learnt from studying your accounts of his adventures that he cannot survive without such challenges. It is you, Doctor, whom I cannot comprehend. I am at a loss to explain your purpose in pursuing this dangerous path. I speak not of your wife's abduction, although why you would jeopardise her safety by remaining upon my trail is a problem in itself. From the beginning you have shown an ungovernable enthusiasm for this chase. Why? What spell has Sherlock Holmes placed upon you that has made you his accomplice in this mad scheme? I have risked everything by coming here, and yet I must have an answer before I return to my homeland."

The reader may think me mad, but in that moment I actually pitied Count Dracula. He was beaten, his destruction was close at hand, and all he wished now was to know why. I answered him without pausing.

"Sherlock Holmes is my friend."

He stood there, blinking, for several seconds after I had spoken. "That is your answer?"

"It is the only one I have. Moreover, it is the correct one."

"I see."

Whether or not he did was something I did not have time to determine, for in that moment there came the sound of hurried footsteps upon the stairs outside the door of the room, and in a flash the vampire left his place and dove headlong through the window, smashing the glass and sending a shower of glittering fragments flying before him. He hit the ground just as the door burst open and Holmes rushed in, followed by the bearded doctor and a half-dozen of the hospital's staff. Holmes's eyes swept the room rapidly and came to rest upon the broken window, to which he bounded and leant out with his hands upon the sill.

"He is gone," he said, straightening. "On his way back to the *Czarina Catherine*, no doubt. Your wife, Watson; he has harmed her?" His expression was anxious.

"No, he did not touch her." I glanced towards her sleeping form and heaved an inward sigh of relief that she had not awakened while the fiend was in the room.

"What did he want?"

I met my friend's gaze calmly. "He wanted to ask a question."

At no time in our long association was the quickness of Holmes's mind more sharply delineated than in the instant following my enigmatic response, for I recognised immediately the signs of comprehension upon his face. His nod of understanding was almost imperceptible.

"And did he receive an answer?"

This time it was my turn to nod.

"What in the name of the devil is going on?" demanded the bearded doctor. He glanced from one to the other of us, his countenance a battlefield upon which anger and bewilderment fought for supremacy. The former won out. "This was a quiet, restful hospital before the pair of you entered it. Suddenly I am forced to stand aside while a madman kicks open the front door and pounds up the stairs and another hurls himself through the window, and then to listen to a pair of jibbering idiots playing word games when I should be healing the sick. I demand an explanation for this outrageous behaviour, or I shall summon the police and let them sort it out. Which shall it be?"

"Steady, Doctor," said Holmes in a placating tone. "Would five pounds replace the damaged window?"

The change that came over the physician's manner when he understood what my friend was saying was a most comical sight. He stood there breathing heavily and opening and closing his mouth like a fish, while the only sounds which ensued reminded me somewhat of an overworked bellows. When at last he found his voice, his rage had been spent, and it was in a much more cordial tone that he addressed himself to the detective.

"Why," he blustered, "five pounds would replace every window upon this floor and pay for a new Bunsen burner besides."

"It is the least we can do to make amends for the disruption which we have engendered." Holmes reached into his pocket. As he did so, an expression of surprise flickered across his face. He tried another pocket, and then another, until there were none left. Finally he turned to me with a most self-deprecating smile.

"Watson, old fellow," he said, "I seem to have run out of funds. Have you five pounds?"

"What happened to the gold coin you found in the slaughter-house?" I asked him.

"I fear that it is at the bottom of the harbour. I had other things to think about during that swim than the contents of my pockets."

I began fumbling among the pockets of my trousers and jacket while the doctor watched, his brow darkening. For a disturbing moment it looked as if my companion and I might be celebrating our victory against Dracula in the dungeons of the local gaol, but at length I succeeded in fishing out a soggy five-pound note and turned it over to the doctor. Holmes's breath came out in a grateful sigh.

"I told you this case was costing us, Watson."

I did not speak with him again until we had said our farewells to Mary and shouldered our way through the hospital staff into the hallway. "Are we going after Dracula?" I asked Holmes on the way down the stairs.

He shook his head. "His ship has sailed by now; the crew was making final preparations when I left the docks. He will not touch ground again until he reaches Varna."

"What is stopping us from taking a train to Varna and resuming our pursuit?"

He stopped at the base of the stairs to light his pipe. Where he had secured dry matches and tobacco at that early hour remains a mystery to this day. "I think, Watson," said he, "that we shall leave that task for Van Helsing and company. Our part in the drama ends here."

I could hardly credit my hearing. "It is not like you to quit a case before it is finished, Holmes," I chastised.

"Oh, but it *is* finished. We have accomplished what we originally set out to do, which was to rescue England from the vampire's clutches. In so doing, we have inadvertently saved America as well. I think that that is enough for two middle-aged men, don't you?"

"But what if you're wrong? What if Van Helsing is unable to trace Dracula back to his homeland? In a year's time the fiend may try again."

"Do not sell the professor short. He is a relentless man. He and his companions will dog Dracula's trail night and day, and they will not give up until they have sent the sanguinary Count to the eternal rest which has been waiting to receive him for over four hundred years. Our reward is the knowledge that it is we who put him on the defensive."

He fell silent as we stepped into the street, which was just beginning to display signs of life as the citizens of Whitby awoke and went about their daily morning routine. Suddenly there was a horrendous clamour from up the street, a clattering of hooves accompanied by clanging bells. Heads swung in that direction.

"What the devil!" I cried.

Presently, an ambulance driven by a man with a flying whip swung around the corner upon two wheels and came to a screeching halt in front of the hospital. It was followed by another, and yet a third, until the entire street was a clutter of what the lower classes term "meat waggons." The driver of the first vehicle leapt to the street and hurried around to the back, where he and his companion who had been ringing the alarm bell tore open the rear doors and pulled out a blanket-wrapped figure lying upon a stretcher.

"What's happened?" Holmes inquired of the driver as he and his partner bore the stretcher between them up the steps of the hospital.

"Shipwreck," snapped the other. "Another one fetched up on the reef last night. Happens every time there's a storm."

"Was anyone killed?" Holmes and I fell into step with them.

"Don't think so. Captain thinks everyone jumped off before she hit, but he's not sure. He's fuzzy about the whole thing." The door closed upon them.

"Hardy souls, these Americans," Holmes commented as we stood aside to let the other attendants pass with their soggy burdens. "They were fortunate the *Baltimore* never reached the open sea, for Dracula had a much worse fate in store for them than drowning."

I heard someone cursing and turned to see a brawny sailor struggling with two attendants who were endeavouring to keep him upon a stretcher. My heart soared when I recognised him.

"Holmes! It's Ned Bridger!"

When he heard his name, Bridger ceased his struggles for a moment and looked up at us from the base of the hospital steps. He sprang to his feet and bounded up to where we were standing, despite the attempts of his keepers to restrain him. "Mr. Holmes!" he cried exultantly. "Am I glad to see you! Tell these blokes I don't want to be tied down to no bed in no hospital. Their hearing's none too good where I'm concerned."

The detective's face was positively aglow. I had not realised until that moment how deeply the sailor's supposed death had affected him. "It seems to be a night for resurrection," he observed. "First myself, then the crew of the clipper, and now you. I would have sworn in a court of law that you did not have time to jump before the boiler blew."

"Aye, and you'd have been right. She must of blown me fifteen feet straight up, but I came down with enough of my senses left to swim to shore." He swung upon me. "Your wife, mate. You got her?"

I nodded. "I got her, thanks to you."

The uniformed attendants were at his side now. He looked pleadingly at Holmes. "Come now, Mr. Holmes," he entreated. "Tell them to go dig up their own corpse. I hate hospitals."

Holmes smiled. "Obviously, you haven't seen the nurses at this particular hospital."

"Nurses?" Bridger grinned. "Pretty, are they? Well, I suppose I could do with a rest." So saying, he locked arms with his escorts and allowed them to usher him through the door.

"I noticed no nurses," I confided to Holmes as we descended the steps to the street. "No female nurses, at any rate."

"Of course you didn't. The staff of Whitby Hospital is one hundred per cent male."

"But you said–"

"I said, 'Obviously, you haven't seen the nurses at this particular hospital.' I said nothing as to their appearance or gender. If our sailor friend construed otherwise, I am not to blame."

The sight of the last of the stricken sailors being carried out of the third ambulance struck a chord in my memory. Suddenly I stopped and seized my friend's arm.

"Holmes!" I exclaimed. "What about the box of earth? Dracula cannot go anywhere without it!"

There was no change in his expression. "Where do you think I was all the time I was absent?" he said. "I knew that he would send someone back to the wreck for it, so I thought to hedge my bet by dumping out its contents before its escort arrived. But Dracula was one step ahead of me as usual; the box was missing when I returned to the *Baltimore.* He has it with him now." He smiled at the disappointment upon my face. "My dear fellow, cheer up. A few hours' rest and a change of clothing–I will send out for what we need–will lift your spirits considerably. By then we should receive further word of Mrs. Watson's condition, and I have a distinctly unanalytical hunch that the news will be good… I assume. you have sufficient cash on hand to secure us a room at the hotel?"

Chapter Fifteen

A New Mystery

It was November, the first since we had driven the nightmare from our shores. Outside the window, the first snowflakes of winter were enjoying a brief moment of glory before being trod into an unrecognisable slush beneath the traffic upon the street. I sat in the armchair in my sitting room nodding over a yellow-backed novel while Mary engaged in a mysterious operation involving a pair of knitting needles and a ball of yarn in the chair opposite. The clock upon the mantelpiece struck ten, bringing me awake, and I had placed my hands upon the arms of my chair preparatory to rising and going up to bed when there was a ring at the door. Mary put down her knitting with a sigh.

"Another patient! And you've had such a long day."

"It seems that it is not over yet," said I, stepping reluctantly towards the door. I opened it to reveal Sherlock Holmes's slender form standing upon my threshold.

"Up late this evening, eh, Watson?"

"Holmes!" I exclaimed happily. "Come in out of that beastly snow! I haven't seen you since–"

"Since the rather amusing affair of Mr. Jabez Wilson and the so-called Red-Headed League," said he, bounding into the room. He was dressed in his travelling clothes, his shoulders and cap heaped with fresh snow. Seeing Mary, he removed his cap. "Ah, there's a sight to warm my soul! What is it this time, Mrs. Watson? An antimacassar? Or a cosy shawl for the doctor's shoulders?"

"Neither," replied Mary, accepting his outstretched hand with a warm smile. "It's a pullover, and it was going to be your Christmas present until you spoiled the surprise."

"Then I shall do my best to forget that I saw it. Thank you, Watson, but I haven't time for brandy. I've a hansom waiting outside and a ship to catch in thirty minutes."

I returned the decanter to the cabinet from which I had taken it and closed the door. "The Continent?" I asked.

He nodded briskly, releasing a cascade of snow from the collar of his coat onto Mary's new carpet. "I've a little matter waiting for me there which may take me some time to clear up. No, no, dear fellow"–he held up a hand to stop me from slipping into my coat–"I wouldn't dream of taking you away from your practice so soon after the last time. There's no use arguing with me because I've made up my mind upon the subject. I merely stopped by to wish you both well and to show you this."

It was a telegram. I unfolded it and read:

ALL IS WELL. HE IS DEAD. FOR SERVICES
UNINVITED, GRATITUDE.
V.H.
VARNA, BULGARIA

"V.H.?" I asked, perplexed.

"Van Helsing. It appears that Dracula's threat is ended. Reluctant though the professor's thanks seem, they are the mark of a big man, and I shall be glad to add his wire to my collection of memorabilia. It is the only souvenir I have to remind me of this case. Not that I need one."

"I did not know that he was aware of our involvement." I gave him back the telegram.

"He knew from the start. I told you before not to underestimate him. How is Mrs. Barton?"

"She is well. I believe she is at Mass tonight."

"Ah! Then her religion is not merely a thing to be relied upon in emergencies. Well, I said she was a devout woman." He swung open the door. "My chariot awaits. The best of holidays, Dr. and Mrs. Watson. I will see you in ninety-one."

"And what will the New Year bring?" I inquired.

He paused upon the threshold and met my gaze. "That, my dear fellow," he said, "is as much a mystery to me as it is to you." And with that he struck off into the snow and the darkness.

Acknowledgements

The task of clarifying and authenticating Watson's manuscript could not have been undertaken but for the aid of three towering examples of Sherlockiana: *The Private Life of Sherlock Holmes* by Vincent Starrett; *In the Footsteps of Sherlock Holmes* by Michael Harrison; and *The Encyclopaedia Sherlockiana* by Jack Tracy. These volumes saved many hours of poring through dusty histories and English travelogues, as they served as invaluable guides to the environment in which the world's first consulting detective lived and worked.

For encouragement and co-operation, the editor's deerstalker is off both to William B. Thompson, who reawakened an interest in Sherlock Holmes long dormant, and to the members of The Arcadia Mixture, Ann Arbor scion of the national Baker Street Irregulars, who kept alive that interest until it bore fruit. A more genial and sympathetic group of lunatics would be difficult to find.

Most helpful during the final stages were the efforts of the Doubleday team, who, in their enthusiasm for "our" book, excelled themselves in order to rid the manuscript of inconsistencies and ambiguities. Those that remain must be charged to the editor alone.

Lastly, the editor wishes to thank his family for their sympathy and understanding during the months of work on the manuscript, to say nothing of numerous suggestions which spared hours of research. Their interest is appreciated.

L.D.E

About the Authors

John H. Watson, M.D., M.B., B.S., M.R.C.S., was born in England in 1852. In 1878 he took his medical degree at the University of London and shortly after served as assistant surgeon with the Fifth Northumberland Fusiliers in Afghanistan. Then he transferred to the Berkshires and was severely wounded in the Battle of Maiwand, after which he left the service and returned to London. While there, he began his long association with Sherlock Holmes, who became the subject of Watson's more than sixty published books and articles. He was knighted for his medical service during the First World War and died in his country home near New Forest in 1940.

Loren D. Estleman is a graduate of Eastern Michigan University and a veteran police-court journalist. Since the publication of his first novel in 1976, he has established himself as a leading writer of both mystery and western fiction. His western novels include Golden Spur Award winner *Aces and Eights*, *Mister St. John*, *The Stranglers*, and *Gun Man.* His Amos Walker, Private Eye series includes *Motor City Blue*,

Angel Eyes, *The Midnight Man*, *The Glass Highway*, Shamus Award-winner *Sugartown*, *Every Brilliant Eye*, *Lady Yesterday*, *Downriver*, and *A Smile on the Face of the Tiger*. Mr. Estleman lives in Michigan with his wife, Deborah, who writes under the name Deborah Morgan.

Also Available

DR. JEKYLL & MR. HOLMES

By LOREN D. ESTLEMAN

Preface

One might think, now that the world is falling down about our ears, that interest in a man whose entire career was with few exceptions dedicated to the eradication of domestic evils would naturally diminish in the face of danger from without. That, however, is not the case. My publishers have for some time been badgering me to dip once again into that battered tin dispatch-box in which I long ago packed away the last of my notes dealing with those singular problems which engaged the gifts of Mr. Sherlock Holmes, and to lay yet another of them before an eager public. For a long time I demurred – not because of any unwillingness upon my part but rather in deference to the wishes of my friend, who has since his retirement repeatedly enjoined me from taking any action to enhance fame which has of late proved cumbersome to him. The reader may imagine my reaction then, when, one day last week, I answered the telephone in my Kensington home and recognised Sherlock Holmes's voice upon the line.

'Good morning, Watson. I trust that you are well.'

'Holmes!'

'Whose call were you anticipating so anxiously, or does that fall under the heading of "most secret"?'

My surprise at being made contact with in this fashion by one for whom the telegraph remained the chief form of communication was heightened by this unexpected and accurate observation.

'How did you know that I was expecting a telephone call?' I asked incredulously.

'Simplicity itself. You answered the infernal device before the first ring was completed.'

'Wonderful! But what brings you to London? I thought that you had retired to the South Downs, this time for good.'

'I am seeing a specialist about my rheumatism. I am afraid that the two years I spent trailing Von Bork did me no service. Have you still in your possession your notes regarding the affair in Soho in '84?'

I was caught off-guard by this seeming irrelevancy. 'Indeed I do,' I responded.

'Excellent. I think that your readers may find some interest in the complete account. Mind you, be kind to Stevenson.'

'The legal question –'

'– is moot, I think, after all these years. Whitehall has far more important things to deal with at present than a thirty-year-old shooting, particularly one committed in self-defence.'

From there he steered the conversation into a discussion of the progress of the war, agreed with me that America's entry into the conflict would spell doom for the Huns, and rang off after a talk of less than three minutes.

Since I have never pretended to any talents in detection, I shall not attempt to fathom his reason for dragging forth this long-buried memory, which would seem to hold little in common with the holocaust in which Europe finds itself at present. I had asked for and been denied permission to publish the facts of that case too many times to question this unexpected boon. To borrow a phrase from the Yanks, I am not inclined towards looking gift horses in the mouth; I shall, therefore, make haste to consult my notebook for the years 1883-85, set down the events as they occurred at the time, and concern myself with my friend's state of mind upon some other occasion.

Holmes's admonition to 'be kind to Stevenson' was unnecessary. Although it is true that Robert Louis Stevenson's account of the singular circumstances surrounding the murder of Sir Danvers Carew contains numerous omissions, it is just as true that discretion, and not slovenliness, obliged him to withhold certain facts and to publish *The Strange Case of Dr. Jekyll and Mr. Hyde* under the guise of fiction. Victorian society simply would not have accepted it in any other form.

Now, after thirty-two years, the full story can at last be told. The pages which follow this preface represent variations upon the theme set forth in Stevenson's largely accurate but incomplete account. As with any two differing points of view, some details, particularly those dealing with time, vary, although not significantly. This is due, no doubt, to the fact that my notes were made upon first-hand observation at the time the events were unfolding, whilst Stevenson's were made upon hearsay at best, months and in some cases years after the fact. I leave the decision concerning whose version is correct to the reader.

As I write these words, it occurs to me that the story is in fact a timely one, in that it demonstrates the evils which a science left to itself may inflict upon an unsuspecting mankind. A culture which allows zeppelins to rain death and destruction upon the cities of men and heavy guns to pound civilisation back into the dust whence it came is a culture which has yet to learn from its mistakes. It is therefore hoped that the chronicle which follows will serve as a lesson to the world that the laws of nature are inviolate, and that the penalty for any attempt to circumvent them is swift and merciless. Assuming, that is, that there will still be a world when the present cataclysm has run its course

John H. Watson, M.D.
London, England
August 6th, 1917.

The Mysterious Beneficiary

'Holmes,' said I, 'I have a cab waiting.'

I was standing in the doorway of our lodgings at 221B Baker Street, hands in the pockets of my ulster and glad of its warmth now that the chill of late October had begun to invade the sitting room in the absence of a fire in the grate. My fellow-lodger, however, appeared oblivious to the cold as he busied himself at the acid-stained deal table in the corner, his long, thin back concealing from me his specific operations. Nearby, studying the proceedings in baffled fascination, stood a broad-shouldered commissionaire in the trim uniform of his occupation.

'One moment, Watson,' said Sherlock Holmes, and executed a quarter-turn round upon his stool so that I might see what he was doing. With the aid of a glass pipette he drew a quantity of bluish liquid from a beaker boiling atop the flame of his Bunsen burner and expelled it into a test tube which he held in his left hand. Then he laid aside the pipette and took up a slip of paper upon which was heaped a small mound of white powder, curling it part way round his thumb so as not to spill any of its contents. His metallic grey eyes were bright with anticipation.

'Purple is the fatal colour, Doctor,' he informed me. 'Should the liquid assume that hue once I have introduced this other substance – as I suspect it will – a murder has been committed and a woman will march to the gallows. Thus!' He tipped the powder into the tube.

The commissionaire and I leant forward to stare at the contents. The powder formed curling patterns as it descended through the liquid, but long before it reached the bottom it dissolved. In its place, a stream of bright bubbles sped to the top and floated there. Holmes drummed the table with impatient fingers, awaiting the expected result.

The liquid retained its bluish tint.

I am not by nature an envious person, and yet, as moment followed upon moment with no change in the colour of the concoction in the tube, I confess that I had all I could do to maintain my countenance in the presence of Holmes's undisguised bewilderment. He seemed so invariably right that I can scarcely describe the elation which I as a mere mortal felt to witness a rare moment of fallibility upon his part, proving that he, too, was subject to the frailties of the race. Fortunately for our relationship, my efforts to control my own mirth became unnecessary when he burst out laughing.

'Well, well,' said he, once he had recaptured his customary calm, 'so the matter is an innocent one after all, and the joke is on me. Well, it's a hazard of the profession, this *penchant* for always looking towards the dark side; if nothing else, I have learnt a most valuable lesson.' He replaced the test tube in its rack, took up a pen and a scrap of paper, scribbled something upon the latter, and handed the message and a coin to the commissionaire. 'Take this to Inspector Gregson, my good man, and tell him that Mr. Wingate Dennis did indeed die a natural death – as the postmortem will undoubtedly reveal – and that Mrs. Dennis is guilty of no more heinous a crime than a perhaps too free use of sugar in her husband's tea. And now, Watson,' said he, as the messenger departed, 'it's you and me for King's Cross Station and the North of England for a well-deserved rest.' He rose from the stool and reached for his hat and coat.

During the early years of our friendship preceding my marriage, and even before I had begun to chronicle our adventures together, Sherlock Holmes's fame as a consulting detective had travelled by word-of-mouth throughout London, and people in distress were turning to him for aid in such volumes that by the autumn of 1883 I became seriously concerned for his health and demanded that he take a holiday. This time, to my surprise – for I had made much the same suggestion upon a number of occasions and been turned down – he readily agreed, and at last our bags were packed and loaded and we had but to descend to ground level and climb aboard the hansom to be off to Nottingham for a month of relaxation far from the ills of the city. Under the circumstances, the reader may understand my chagrin when, just as we were heading for the door, our landlady came in with a card upon her salver and announced that we had a visitor.

'"G. J. Utterson",' Holmes read, taking up the card. 'Did you explain to Mr. Utterson that we are leaving, Mrs. Hudson?'

'I did, Mr. Holmes, but the gentleman said that his business is urgent.'

'Very well, then, send him up. And please be good enough to ask the cabby to wait a bit longer.' He turned a rueful face upon me. 'I am truly sorry, my dear fellow, but as a doctor you will agree that turning one's back upon a brother human being in need is hardly the act of a responsible practitioner.'

'As a doctor,' said I curtly, 'I can only warn that you are courting grave danger.'

He removed his outer garments and returned them to their hook. 'It is the price I pay for being the only one of my kind. But pray, put up your own coat and hat and prepare to assume your favourite seat, for

I judge by our visitor's troubled footfall that he will welcome an extra pair of sympathetic ears.'

Presently the door opened again and a grave-visaged gentleman was ushered into our quarters. In appearance he was between forty and fifty years of age, leaning towards the latter, and was dressed most impeccably in a dark suit and topcoat with a quiet check. On his boots he sported a pair of neat gaiters, but since these were not in keeping with the soberness of the rest of his attire I gathered that they had been donned more for protection than for style, as a light rain had been falling over London throughout the day and puddles were numerous. I have mentioned that his visage was grave, but as he stepped farther into the light cast by the single lamp we had left burning, the similarities between it and the face of a professional mourner grew sharp. Long, rugged, scored across the brow with creases of worry, it might have belonged to an aged bloodhound but for a modest black moustache and greying hair carefully arranged and pomaded to conceal a balding pate. His eyes too were sad, but with a genuine sorrow that could only have been the result of deepest despair. My heart had never gone out to a complete stranger as swiftly as it went out to Mr. G. J. Utterson even before he opened his mouth to speak.

He waited until Mrs. Hudson had withdrawn, closing the door behind her, then looked from one to the other of us as if uncertain which man to address first.

'Good afternoon, Mr. Utterson,' Holmes opened, offering his hand, which was reservedly accepted. 'I am Sherlock Holmes and this is my companion, Dr. Watson, in whom you may place whatever confidence you extend to me. I shan't ask you to remove your coat – it is, after all, chilly in here without a fire – but there is a chair; I suggest that you take it, for you must be exhausted after walking about London most of the day.'

Our visitor had been in the act of seating himself in the chair which we set aside for prospective clients; at Holmes's final remark he paused in some astonishment, then dropped into it as though weakened by a physical blow. 'However did you ascertain that?' he stammered. 'What you say is true, but I cannot imagine how –'

'Common observation,' interrupted my friend, offering the newcomer a cigar from his case, which was declined. 'Your trousers are liberally splashed with various kinds of mud from different parts of the city. They reach rather higher than they would have had you been traveling in, say, a hansom or a four-wheeler; hence my deduction that you were walking. That you have been doing so for the best part of the day is evident by the variety of the splashes, indicating that you covered a great deal of ground in your meanderings. There is also a dried crust upon the left side of the crown of your hat – precipitated there, most likely, by the hand of some ruffian in the East End, which from the quality of your attire I should judge to be somewhat removed from your usual surroundings.'

Mr. Utterson looked down at the top hat resting upon his knee, the band of which was indeed encrusted with dirt upon one side. 'My hat was dislodged by a handful of mud hurled by a filthy little chimney sweep in Houndsditch, but a wave of my stick put him to flight. In another moment I suppose you will tell me his name.'

'You flatter me beyond my abilities,' said Holmes. But his cheeks flushed at the compliment. He sank into his beloved armchair and stretched his long legs out before the nonexistent fire. 'I should like to hear a statement of your problem, Mr. Utterson, which my landlady informs me is of some moment. I beg you to lay it before me exactly as you would prepare any case for a magistrate. Oh, no more praise, if you please' – here he raised a hand – 'that sheaf of legal documents protruding from your inside breast pocket could only belong to an lawyer. I recognise a telltale Latin phrase here and there among its text.'

At the mention of his profession, our visitor had shot bolt upright, gripping the arms of his chair, but as Holmes explained the simple steps by which he had arrived at his conclusion, he relaxed, though not so completely as he might have done were he at home in his own sitting room. I knew from prior experience how unsettling it was to be in the presence of a man before whom one's life was an open book.

'If it please you, sir,' he said, 'I think I have use for that cigar which you offered me earlier.'

The case being out of Holmes's reach, I picked it up and pushed it across to the lawyer. He selected a cigar, snipped the end off fastidiously with a silver clipper on the end of his watch-chain, shook his head politely to my offer of a match, and lit it with one of his own.

'Your name, Mr. Holmes, was given me by my cousin, Mr. Richard Enfield, who engaged your services some time ago in a matter involving the disappearance of a rare coin which had been entrusted to his care. He told me that you were a man upon whose confidence I could rely absolutely.'

Holmes caught my eye and wiggled a finger in the direction of his desk. I caught his meaning and, after unlocking and opening the drawer, drew out his small case-book and brought it over to him.

'Thank you, Watson,' said he, flipping through the pages. 'Enfield. Here it is.' He read swiftly and closed the book. 'I remember the case. An 1813 guinea, stamped twice by accident, resulting in a double image of George III. He was holding it for a friend. It was not stolen at all, but merely misplaced. I found it inside the velvet lining of the box in which it was kept.' He held up the book, which I returned to the drawer and locked away. 'Would that all of life's difficulties were as easily resolved, eh, Mr. Utterson?'

The other nodded in grave agreement. 'I fear that the problem which

I bring does not fall into that category.' He leant forward in his chair. 'Please do not think it an insult, but I must stress the value – nay, the necessity – of secrecy in this affair. It must not go beyond this room.'

'You have my promise,' said Holmes.

'And mine,' said I.

Our responses seemed to satisfy him, for he nodded again and sat back, puffing at his cigar.

'My oldest client and dearest friend,' he began, 'is a man by the name of Dr. Henry Jekyll, about whom you may have heard. His name is not unknown among circles both social and scientific.'

'I am familiar with his reputation,' said I.

'Then you know that he has been deemed brilliant by a number of our leading medical journals for the great strides which he has made in that field through his research. He is moreover a decent man, to whom friendship is no idle word but a sacred bond, to be preserved at the cost of life itself. Some time ago, however, he came to me with a most unsettling request having to do with his last will and testament.'

'Excuse me,' broke in the detective. 'How old a man is Dr. Jekyll?'

'He is nearing the half-century mark, as indeed am I.'

'Is that not the age at which a man begins seriously to contemplate his own mortality?'

'It is not his wish to draw up a will which upset me,' said the other. 'Rather, it was the terms which he dictated. Shall I show you the document?' He reached inside his coat and drew forth a packet of papers, which he proceeded to unfold.

'Would you not be betraying a confidence if you did?' asked my friend.

'I would rather be deprived of the privilege to practise law because of an indiscretion than lose a friend as close as Henry Jekyll, for it is for his life that I fear.'

'Then pray, summarise the terms. My Latin grows rustier by the day.'

The lawyer donned a pair of gold-rimmed spectacles to consult the paper which he held in his hands. 'Briefly, they add up to the following: In the event of Henry Jekyll's death, disappearance, or unexplained absence for any period to exceed three calendar months, all of his worldly possessions – some two hundred and fifty thousand pounds sterling – are to pass into the hands of a gentleman by the name of Edward Hyde.' He refolded the document and returned it, along with his spectacles, to his pocket. 'Mr. Holmes, have you ever in your life heard of such terms?'

'They are singular, to say the least. Who is this Edward Hyde?'

'That is the mystery which has brought me to you. I never heard of the man before Jekyll named him as beneficiary.'

'You questioned Jekyll?'

'He said only that he had a special interest in the young man. I could draw him out no further.'

'Is that all the information you can supply?'

'There is a second part to my story. I mentioned my cousin, Richard Enfield, earlier. He is a gadabout and something of a gossip, but I find his company refreshing after hours of seclusion with dry paperwork. It was during our constitutional a week ago Sunday that he related to me the details of an incident which have left me virtually sleepless these past eleven nights.

'He told me that he was on his way home from some revel in the wee hours of a winter morning when he chanced to witness a collision involving two pedestrians at a nearby corner. One, a little, dwarf-like man, was hurrying along towards the corner whilst the other, a very young girl, was running at top speed at right angles to him, neither being aware of the other's presence until the moment of impact. It was a commonplace occurrence; a blustering apology would usually ensue if the man was a gentleman, or, if he was not, a sharp word – one could hardly expect more. But the girl fell, and before she could get to her feet this brute trampled right over her, oblivious to her cries and proceeding as if she were the merest pile of debris round which he had not the time to walk. A shocking scene, as Enfield described it.'

'I should say so!' I blurted out, unable to control my reaction to such uncivilised behaviour in the age of Victoria.

Utterson continued, ignoring my comment. 'The ruffian might have escaped, for his pace was swift, but Enfield's stride was longer and he collared him at the corner. By that time the girl's family had arrived and the local physician was summoned, and though by God's grace the child was unharmed, their anger was such that they might have fallen upon the offender and torn him to pieces then and there had not my cousin held them back through sheer force of reason. This was more out of respect for human life upon his part than from any sympathy towards the ruffian, who seemed to inspire a strange revulsion in whoever glimpsed his face beneath the lamplight, including Enfield himself. A blackguard of the most obvious sort, this fellow, was the impression I got.

'In lieu of his life, or at the very least a session in court, the ruffian agreed to surrender the sum of a hundred pounds to the girl's family, and led them presently to the door of a shabby building on a by-street in one of the city's busier quarters, whereupon he asked his escort to wait whilst he produced a key and went in. Some moments later he returned with a purse containing ten pounds in gold and a cheque for the balance, drawn upon the account of a man well known to Enfield. Of course they didn't trust it, so at the ruffian's suggestion they spent the night in my cousin's chambers until the bank opened in the morning and they were able to cash the cheque without incident. After which the fellow was released.'

'An ugly episode,' said Holmes, 'but hardly illuminating. What is its connexion with the matter which we are discussing?'

'The strangest, Mr. Holmes.' Utterson chewed the end of his cigar nervously. It was plain that he was keeping himself in check with an effort. 'When the story was told to me, we were standing across the street from the very door through which the ruffian had passed to fetch the money and the cheque. Enfield pointed it out. It is a side entrance to the home of Dr. Henry Jekyll, and the cheque was made out upon his account to the order of the bearer, Edward Hyde.'

'Good Lord!' I cried.

Holmes, who had listened to Utterson's story thus far in the somnolent attitude which he assumed whenever the facts of a new case were stated to him, sat up suddenly, steely eyes flashing. For the space of a heartbeat he and the lawyer stared at each Other in silence.

'Dismiss the cab, Watson,' said Holmes finally.

the further adventures of
SHERLOCK HOLMES
THE TITANIC TRAGEDY
THE WORLD'S GREATEST DETECTIVE RETURNS
WILLIAM SEIL

the further adventures of
SHERLOCK HOLMES
THE WEB WEAVER
THE WORLD'S GREATEST DETECTIVE RETURNS
SAM SICILIANO

the further adventures of
SHERLOCK HOLMES
THE STAR OF INDIA
THE WORLD'S GREATEST DETECTIVE RETURNS
CAROLE BUGGÉ

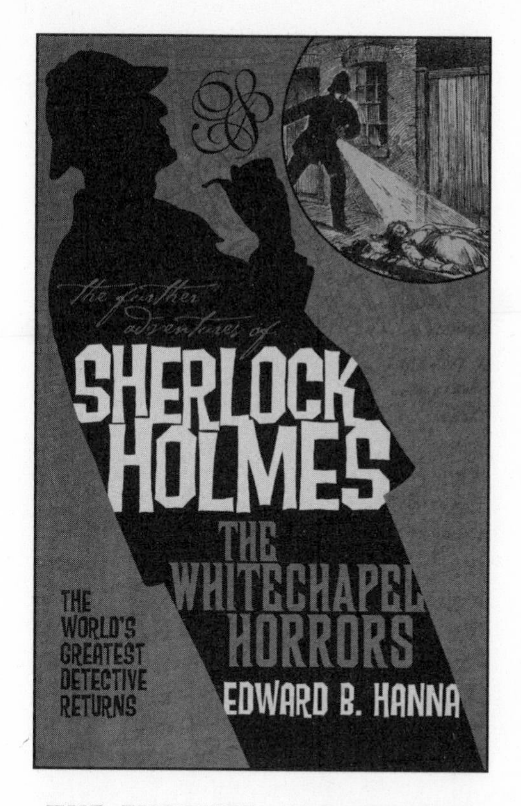

THE FURTHER ADVENTURES OF SHERLOCK HOLMES

THE WHITECHAPEL HORRORS

Edward B. Hanna

Grotesque murders are being committed on the streets of Whitechapel. Sherlock Holmes believes he knows the identity of the killer–Jack the Ripper. But as he delves deeper, Holmes realizes that revealing the murderer puts much more at stake than just catching a killer…

ISBN: 9781848567498

AVAILABLE NOW!

the further adventures of
SHERLOCK HOLMES
DR. JEKYLL & MR. HOLMES
THE WORLD'S GREATEST DETECTIVE RETURNS
LOREN D. ESTLEMAN

THE FURTHER ADVENTURES OF SHERLOCK HOLMES

THE SEVENTH BULLET

Daniel D. Victor

Sherlock Holmes and Dr. Watson travel to New York City to investigate the assassination of true-life muckraker and author David Graham Phillips. They soon find themselves caught in a web of deceit, violence and political intrigue, which only the great Sherlock Holmes can unravel.

ISBN: 9781848566767

AVAILABLE NOW!

SHERLOCK HOLMES

THE ARMY OF DR MOREAU

Guy Adams

Dead bodies are found on the streets of London with wounds that can only be explained as the work of ferocious creatures not native to the city.

Sherlock Holmes is visited by his brother, Mycroft, who is only too aware that the bodies are the calling card of Dr Moreau, a vivisectionist who was working for the British Government, following in the footsteps of Charles Darwin, before his experiments attracted negative attention and the work was halted. Mycroft believes that Moreau's experiments continue and he charges his brother with tracking the rogue scientist down before matters escalate any further.

A brand-new original novel, detailing a thrilling new case for the acclaimed detective Sherlock Holmes.

SHERLOCK HOLMES

THE BREATH OF GOD

Guy Adams

The nineteenth century is about to draw to a close. In its place will come the twentieth, a century of change, a century of science, a century that will see the superstitions of the past swept away.
There are some who are determined to see that never happens.

A body is found crushed to death in the London snow. There are no footprints anywhere near it. It is almost as if the man was killed by the air itself. This is the first in a series of attacks that sees a handful of London's most prominent occultists murdered. While pursuing the case, Sherlock Holmes and Dr. Watson find themselves traveling to Scotland to meet with the one person they have been told can help: Aleister Crowley.

As dark powers encircle them, Holmes' rationalist beliefs begin to be questioned. The unbelievable and unholy are on their trail as they gather a group of the most accomplished occult minds in the country: Doctor John Silence, the so-called "Psychic Doctor"; supernatural investigator Thomas Carnacki; runic expert and demonologist Julian Karswell...

But will they be enough? As the century draws to a close it seems London is ready to fall and the infernal abyss is growing wide enough to swallow us all.

A brand-new original novel, detailing a thrilling new case for the acclaimed detective Sherlock Holmes.

PROFESSOR MORIARTY

THE HOUND OF THE D'URBERVILLES

Kim Newman

Imagine the twisted evil twins of Holmes and Watson and you have the dangerous duo of Professor James Moriarty–wily, snake-like, fiercely intelligent, terrifyingly unpredictable–and Colonel Sebastian 'Basher' Moran–violent, politically incorrect, debauched. Together they run London crime, owning police and criminals alike.

A one-stop shop for all things illegal, from murder to high-class heists, Moriarty and Moran have a stream of nefarious visitors to their Conduit Street rooms, from the Christian zealots of the American West, to the bloodthirsty Si Fan and *Les Vampires* of Paris, as well as a certain Miss Irene Adler...

"It's witty, often hilarious stuff. The author portrays the scurrilous flipside of Holmes's civil ordered world, pokes fun at 'guest stars' from contemporary novels and ventures into more outré territory than Conan Doyle even dared."
Financial Times

"*The Hound of the d'Ubervilles* is a clever, funny mash-up of a whole range of literary sources including Thomas Hardy, HG Wells, EW Hornung, Maurice Leblanc and most of all, Conan Doyle's Sherlock Holmes stories and novels... It is extravagantly gruesome, gothic and grotesque."
The Independent